How to Steal the Pharaoh's Jewels

A Thief in Love Suspense Romance, Volume 2

Cailin Briste

Hot Sauce Publishing

HOW TO STEAL THE PHARAOH'S JEWELS

Image/art disclaimer: Licensed material is being used for illustrative purposes only. Any person depicted in the licensed material is a model.

ISBN-13 978-0-9989125-3-0
Cover Artist: Cailin Briste
Published in the United States of America

Hot Sauce Publishing
PO Box 13508
Offutt AFB, NE 68113-0508
www.hotsaucepublishing.com

This e-book is a work of fiction. While reference might be made to actual historical events or existing locations, the names, characters, places and incidents are either the product of the author's imagination or are used fictitiously, and any resemblance to actual persons, living or dead, business establishments, events, or locales is entirely coincidental.

Warning

This e-book contains sexually explicit scenes and adult language and may be considered offensive to some readers. Hot Sauce Publishing's e-books are for sale to adults ONLY, as defined by the laws of the country in which you made your purchase. Please store your files wisely, where they cannot be accessed by under-aged readers.

CAILIN BRISTE

DEDICATION

For my girls who have always brought me joy from the moment they came into my life.

Acknowledgments

To Szarka Carter for spending hours helping me figure out the value of the Pharaoh's jewels. Your expertise and willingness to share are always a wonder.

To Lea Schafer for pointing me in the right direction and insisting I do better.

To Samantha at Proofreading By the Page for her marvelous ability to proofread.

To the members of Cailin's Romance Immersion Therapy Facebook group for your encouragement.

To Dr. K for reading the entire manuscript more than once and bringing me tea and toast when I especially needed it. I love you.

CHAPTER ONE

CADE KISSED THE SIDE of Bassinae's head. "Why do you watch these things if they scare you so much? You're practically in my lap."

"I like it. Besides"—she grasped his hand to pull his arm tighter—"I have you to keep me safe."

"Always." He gave her a squeeze. "But protective detail has made me hungry. You promised to feed me if I watched this horror vid with you."

She slapped his thigh. "And a promise is a promise. I can make sandwiches, or we can go to Gio's."

"Let's stay in. Eat on the terrace. This is the nicest day we have had so far this year."

"Sandwiches it is."

He followed her into the kitchen, opening the cooler door to grab a brew. "How do you find anything in this mess?"

"My apartment may be cluttered, but I know where everything is." She took the handle from him and opened the door wider. "What do you want?"

"A beer. If there's one hiding amid all those bottles of health drinks."

She reached in and pulled out the beverage he'd been looking for and handed it to him, pushing him away from the cooler when he reached out to rearrange things. "Oh no you don't. You can turn your cooler into a military barracks, not mine. Get to the terrace. I'll bring our sandwiches out in a minute."

"Fine. But none of those disgusting kelp chips."

If he had seen the broad grin on her face, he would have scowled and accused her of plotting to poison him with health food. Instead he sauntered out of the kitchen toward the terrace doors, as always, comfortable with who he was. He was her best friend, one of a very short list of men she loved. Purely platonic. Romance was out of the question, but if she were looking for that kind of love, Cade Johnson was the type of man she would look for. He was her biggest supporter, the person she spent most of her time off with.

She turned with a happy sigh to plop slices of bread on the plates she'd placed on the counter. From ingredients she pulled from the cooler, she created a sandwich piled high with Cade's favorites, to which she added a sprinkling of cruciferous vegetable powder that he would never notice. She wouldn't have to resort to these interventions if he ate better, but he refused to eat broccoli, cabbage, cauliflower, or anything he included in his nasty veggies list.

On the terrace she found him stretched out on the one chaise lounge she owned. She handed him his plate. "Hey. That's my spot."

"You snooze, you lose."

"Uh-huh." She gave him the stink eye, but he was already biting into the sandwich. "I'll be right back." When she returned, she scooted a chair toward the chaise, settled in with her own lunch, and propped her bare feet on his leg.

He smirked at her. "That works."

Quiet surrounded them. The sunny balcony with its riot of flowering plants hanging in baskets and standing in clusters of pots was an inviting space to enjoy a lazy afternoon. When the weather allowed, Bassinae often ate her lunch outside, soaking up vitamin D from the sun and letting the warmth seep into her bones.

Cade finished his food before she did, following the last bite with a deep pull from his beer. He shut his eyes and would have been asleep in minutes if she hadn't spoken.

"I've been thinking."

He peered at her with one eye. "And?"

She gazed off into the distance. "I feel like I need something more in my life. I don't know. I love my job, working with abused women at

Do It Now, but it's pretty much a routine. I'm not stretching, growing." She returned her gaze to him. "Does that make sense?"

A furrow appeared on his forehead. "You want to find a new job? You'd have to give up your apartment here. It would be harder to meet you for lunch when I'm free."

"No." She nudged him with her foot. "Not a new job. It's just...something's missing. Maybe I should take up aikido. I don't know. I thought you might have some ideas."

He studied her. "A vacation. That's what you need. Your brain's been sending you subliminal messages ever since Jeanne and Cheyenne left on their beach trip. I've got time coming to me. We could go bake ourselves too." He sliced the air with his hand. "No, we could go hiking in the Béarn Mountains. The two of us. Pack in our supplies. What do you say?" He wiggled his eyebrows at her. "Fresh mountain air. Bubbling streams. A handsome companion."

"It sounds like fun. I'd go even if you weren't handsome."

A triumphant grin broke across his face. "Ah-ha! The truth at last. She thinks I'm handsome."

She threw a kelp chip at him. "Idiot."

It slid off his arm when he flinched away from it. "Watch it, or I'll have you charged with assault with deadly food." He resettled himself and closed his eyes. "Think about it. It could be fun."

Maybe, but it didn't ring true as the solution to what ailed her. Not that she could figure out what was causing this dissonance that had infiltrated her being. She'd become a static creature, good at what she did, but with no new challenges. If only she could lie back and enjoy life the way Cade did. Sometimes she wanted to crawl into his arms and soak in his peaceful confidence.

Sipping from her bottle of green tea lemonade, she contemplated Cade. Maybe he was right and all she really needed was a vacation. Maybe, maybe, maybe. She had more maybes than answers, but she was determined to figure this out.

* * * *

The main thruway to the spaceport was snarled in gridlock, so Cade diverted the car to a slower but better regulated side street. He made this trip frequently enough that he had the route and its alternates memorized, down to the timing of the automated signals. Still he would have preferred the quicker course of an open thruway.

His conversation with Bassinae yesterday replayed in his mind. Was she really so dissatisfied with her life that she'd quit her job at Do It Now? What would that mean for her role as a member of Sebastian's burglary team? Hell, what would it mean to no longer have his best friend and the most important woman in his life right next door? Fate couldn't be that cruel.

And now this road was jammed two intersections ahead.

"Damn traffic!" He slapped his palm on the padded steering wheel. In the old days no one got in his way. But then he'd been wearing battle armor as a peacekeeper for the United Colonies. Nothing like fear to clear citizens from your path.

"Problem?" The deep voice resonating from the back seat was Sebastian St. Croix, Cade's boss and the man who had taken Cade in when the military cast him on the trash heap.

"No. Intersection's blocked ahead. I'll go another street right. We'll get there in plenty of time."

"Do what you have to. You know how my mother hates to stand around and wait. If we're not there, she'll take a cab, and I'll hear about it for the next two weeks."

Cade chuckled. "I'll try to keep you out of trouble." Sebastian's mother was a force of nature. Nothing stopped her from doing as she pleased except for her husband, Sebastian's father. The man was the immovable object that, when necessary, blocked her irresistible drive forward. The only time Cade had been a witness to such a set down, his admiration for the man's authority had grown immensely. But Gerald St. Croix was the only person alive who had that effect on his wife.

The woman refused to use shuttle flights on the planet, even though she was wealthy enough to afford them. One should never take to the air when traveling short distances. This was her dictum based in theory on energy savings. Not that there was any substantial difference in fuel cost between ground and shuttle traffic. She'd grown up on a colony planet that had suffered near-catastrophic power loss from the shoddy infrastructure installed by political crooks. To this day she insisted on saving energy when it didn't overly hinder her pampered lifestyle. Thus, collecting her from the spaceport took an hour-long drive rather than a fifteen-minute flight.

Cade grunted his approval and noted that the route change had worked. The road ahead was less congested, so he relaxed back into his seat and picked up speed. A parking garage lined the left side of the street, with office buildings on the right. He checked the time and glanced in the rearview mirror. "Want some music?"

At that moment, a large dump truck came barreling out of an exit of the parking garage they were about to pass. Cade swung right and hit the brakes hard, hoping to lessen the inevitable impact. The screech of metal and the splintering of the car's plasti-shell filled Cade's ears along with a sound like the roaring thunder of thousands of wild animals stampeding toward him.

Safety foam inundated the foot wells of the car, and the air ballasts deployed. One thought struck him. *No pain.* And then the world winked out.

The next he knew, someone was shouting his name and agony radiated from his pelvis. The gray airbags that held him in place deflated. Before him the mangled remains of the windshield gave him a partially obstructed view of the front end of the dump truck, an irresistible force that even Gerald St. Croix couldn't have stopped. The left side of the car was crushed and had been pushed into the passenger side, displacing Cade two-and-a-half feet to his right.

A voice sounded behind him. "Cade. We're going to get you out of there. Hang on. They'll have to cut you out."

That was Sebastian. *Thank the gods he's okay.* Minutes passed, but it seemed like hours before Cade heard sirens approaching.

"The police and emergency services are here. It's going to be all right, Cade."

How the fuck did this happen? Who in their right mind would drive a dump truck at that speed out of a parking garage onto a street?

"Sir? Can you hear me, sir?" A uniformed man's head and shoulders appeared outside the shattered front window.

"Yes," Cade croaked.

"I'm going to stabilize your neck with a collar and cover you while we break the side window and remove the roof of the vehicle." The man pushed his way farther into the car. He slipped the collar around Cade's neck and secured it, asking, "Where do you hurt?"

"Pelvis."

"Can you tell me what happened?"

"Yeah." Cade mumbled the brief details.

"Okay. We're ready to remove the car's roof. I'm going to place a blanket over you and then a shield. I'll be right here with you." Cade felt the emergency tech take hold of his hand. "It's going to be noisy. If you need us to stop for any reason, squeeze my hand. Got that?"

"Got it. Squeeze your hand. Just get it done. It hurts like hell."

"Pain meds have to wait for a full eval. But as soon as possible we'll get you feeling better."

"I know the drill." Did he ever. Battle armor didn't prevent everything, and even when it worked, the human inside could get battered and bruised.

"Here comes the blanket." With the cover and then the flexible plastic shield in place, Cade's world narrowed further. Claustrophobia enveloped him. He began to pant and grew dizzy.

The emergency med tech's response was muffled but audible. "You're all right. Breathe in slowly through your nose and out through your mouth."

Cade heard the tinkle of falling plasti-glass. His fist clenched, he followed the tech's instructions and the light-headedness passed. Gods. I'm such a limp dick. Hell of a thing for a former special-forces operative to get his nuts handed to him over. Can't take having a blanket covering your head.

Shouting voices intermingled with a whirring sound and then a high, metallic screech, a pause, and then more screaming synthsteel.

The pain in his pelvis became white-hot when something jarred the vehicle. He gritted his teeth as a wave of nausea hit him. His eyelids squeezed shut, he counted seconds. When he reached one hundred forty-eight, light struck his lids, and he opened his eyes.

A long, slender nozzle came into view, releasing a mist on top of the solidified foam that held him in place from the knees down. The foam melted away. He moved his right foot; the other refused to budge. He immediately regretted the action when pain sliced through his torso, down his legs, and up his spine. He struggled to endure the blinding agony, hanging on, waiting for it to ease while he remained frozen, panting in short, staccato breaths. *It's a broken pelvis at the very least. Internal bleeding if it's bad. Hell, it feels like my whole left side is crushed.* He fought the urge to push his way out of the car. *I could be bleeding out. If they don't hurry, I could die.*

The men working over him issued orders for placement of the backboard and the plan for extracting him. Their voices slowly faded into the background as cold gripped him. *Stay awake. Don't pass out. Don't die.* But his body ignored him.

One last image passed through his mind before consciousness winked away: Bassinae.

* * * *

Bassinae watched the sixteen women working in pairs before her move in slow motion through the technique she had just taught them. They were of varying sizes, shapes, and ages, but they all had one thing in common. They had been abused and sought shelter at Do It Now. Bassinae's part of the program was to help them get in shape and teach them how to defend themselves.

The hour for her basic self-defense class was up. "That's all for today ladies. Good effort, everyone. We'll continue to work on that last technique in our next session. Tomorrow is a rest-and-absorb day. Spend time mentally working through each movement of your body for what we've covered so far."

The women broke ranks, talking as they made their way out of the exercise room, offering Bassinae a wave or a nod as they left. She released her thin dreads to fall around her shoulders from the tie holding them off her face. An incoming comm flashed a telltale signal in her mind. She answered the call.

"Hey, it's Bassinae."

"There's been an accident." Even though her voice was thick with emotion, Darcelle St. Croix was easy to recognize.

"Who? What—"

"Cade was driving Sebastian to collect his mother at the spaceport. They were hit by a truck."

Oh my gods. From her head, down her arms and torso to her feet, adrenaline sent a cascade of sensation as every nerve in her body rang out alarm bells.

"Sebastian is okay, but Cade was badly hurt. They had to cut him out of the car."

Cade. Gods, no. No no no. "How bad?" She sank her teeth into her lip hard enough to draw blood.

"I don't know for sure, but Sebastian called to tell me. Max is taking me, and I thought you would want to come." Leave it to Darcelle to be matter-of-fact during a crisis.

For a moment Bassinae was dizzy, unable to think straight, but one thing was certain, nothing would keep her from being there for Cade at the hospital. She was going to have to focus like Darcelle, not let thoughts of the worst defeat her. "I do. I want to come. I'm at Do It Now, but I'm finished for the day. I'll meet you in the garage. Bye."

She looked down at her clothes, tight leggings and a cropped, sleeveless workout top. No time to change. She dashed to the staff break room, grabbed her jacket and messenger bag, and hurried to the elevator that would take her from this secret floor of Sebastian St. Croix's high-rise. Darcelle and Max would come from the penthouse.

The guard stationed by the elevator, Percy, looked grim but gave her a brief commiserating nod. The doors opened at once for a change when she placed her hand on the security panel. Inside she drummed her fingers against her thighs, waiting to drop the sixty-seven stories to the garage level, worrying her lip with her teeth. Cade was tough, former Special Forces, but still... hit by a truck. She'd only known him

14

a few years. He served Sebastian as his bodyguard, driver, and handyman. Not that Cade was good with household projects. No, his kind of handy had more to do with getting things done that skirted the law. Like the ninjas of old, you never saw Cade coming unless he wanted you to. Sebastian had adopted them both into his personal cadre of repossession experts, thieves who stole from thieves.

The backs of her eyes prickled with tears, but she would not cry. In the years since she'd worked at Do It Now, she'd grown stronger. This was no time to fall apart. Cade needed her. Cade, who had been bristly and defensive much of his first year, as though he was compelled to prove himself, to wipe away the taint of his past. But like the mouse who'd pulled the thorn from the lion's paw, she never had to deal with his swipes. Perhaps he'd recognized another wounded soul, but it was more likely that she always returned his roars with her own brand of sweet sunshine. He liked to call her Miss Mary Sunshine. She'd tamed him, and they'd become good friends.

The elevator dropped her in the foyer of the garage. A second bulky security guard, one Bassinae had seen on duty at Do It Now, stood keeping watch, his back against the wall where he could view the entire garage level through the floor-to-ceiling windows that separated the foyer from the parking pads.

"Hi, Dave."

"Ma'am."

Why is security here too? This isn't normal. *"Has there been a threat to Do It Now?"*

He directed his somber gaze at her. "No, ma'am. Security has been beefed up because of the accident." He returned to scanning the garage.

"Oh." Before she could follow with another question, the elevator pinged. Darcelle emerged with Max following her. Her billows of red-brown curls had been tamed into a tight bun, and she wore casual slacks and a sweater. She and Max both bore taut expressions. Max had been with Sebastian since he was a boy. He claimed the gray at his temples and in his short beard were Sebastian's fault.

His words terse, Max said, "We're taking the armored rover." He and Darcelle rushed out the swinging door and toward the row of vehicles parked on the right, opposite the service bays.

Bassinae trotted beside Darcelle. "Why the armored rover? For that matter, why the extra security for an accident? Is there a threat?"

A muscle flexed in Darcelle's jaw. "Maybe. We don't know. There are suspicious aspects to the crash."

Bassinae's mind reeled. *Suspicious aspects? Is someone trying to kill Sebastian?* She climbed into the back seat of the vehicle and leaned forward. "Why don't you believe it was just an accident?"

"Strap in." The order came from Max as he backed the rover out of its space and headed toward the garage's main exit, where another security guard was in place.

Her hands trembled as she fought with the locking mechanism. Had someone discovered Sebastian's side business? Did one of the people he'd stolen from discover who was behind the theft? A few of his victims had strong connections to the crime syndicates on planet and even in the Federation.

"There was no one driving the truck that hit them," Darcelle said over her shoulder.

"Maybe the driver ran off."

Darcelle's voice was harsh. "No. Sebastian looked straight into the cab. No one was driving or even in the vehicle. It was on auto-drive. Someone or something had to jimmy with the programming to cause that accident."

Bassinae fell back against her seat. Auto-drive trucks had multiple fail-safes that kept them moving at a snail's pace. There should have been no way for Cade to miss seeing one coming at them. Her heart rate sped up, and the trembling washed into other parts of her body. *Damn it. No.* She gritted her teeth and fisted her hands. *I will not have a panic attack. Cade is going to be just fine.*

The hours that followed were a nightmare of pacing and waiting. Halfway through surgery a nurse came out to give them an update.

Although they all surrounded him, the nurse directed his information to Sebastian. "Mr. Johnson was suffering from a high volume of blood loss when he arrived in the trauma center. He was perilously close to organ failure, but the paramedics got him to us in time. They'd already placed him in a pelvic wrap, and that probably saved his life."

Bassinae jammed her freezing fingers into her armpits, dropped her chin to her chest, and squeezed her eyes shut, trying to catch her breath while the nurse continued.

"The doctors have stopped the bleeding and transfused him with a combination of synthetic blood and circulatory healing nanites."

Sebastian interrupted. "Will they complete the repair during this surgery?"

"Yes, sir. The trauma surgeons are currently making repairs to the patient's bowel and bladder. Then the orthopedic surgeon will realign and bond his broken pelvic bones. A previous injury makes it a little more complicated, but the doctor says Mr. Johnson should recuperate well."

That statement brought Bassinae's full attention to the nurse. She brushed away the tear trickling down her cheek.

"How much longer will it take?"

The question had been on the tip of Bassinae's own tongue before Sebastian spoke.

"We should have him in recovery in two hours. Once he's settled, I'll let you know. The surgeons will be out to speak with you after that." The nurse looked straight at Bassinae. "He's going to be fine."

Max put his arm around her and drew her back to the waiting-room seats. She laid her head on his shoulder, more tears streaming down her face.

Three hours later after Cade was awake in recovery and the surgeons had filled in the surgery details for them and answered their questions, Bassinae could finally see for herself that Cade was okay.

He lay with his eyes closed, paler than she'd ever seen him. There was a bruise on his cheek and more on his left arm. Quietly she slipped next to the bed and slid her hand into his. His eyelids fluttered open, and he smiled weakly at her. "Miss Mary. Where's that smile of yours? I don't look that bad, do I?"

"You look wonderful." She blinked back more tears.

His fingers stirred, stroking her palm. "You said you needed a new challenge. Your wish is my command. You can whip me into shape again."

She scowled at him. "This is not what I meant. You nearly died, you know."

"Not me. I'd never leave you like that."

Her eyes narrowed. "See that you don't."

He gave her an imploring look. "Give me a kiss. I need some sugar."

She bent to place a quick peck on his mouth but lingered over the warm sweetness of his lips.

When she pulled away, he gazed at her, his eyes dreamy. "That's all the medicine I need."

For a second it seemed like the world shifted under her feet. In a voice she hoped didn't sound as falsely cheerful to Cade as it did to her own ears, she said, "You'll have to work hard if you expect to get more of that."

Darcelle poked her head in the door. "Knock, knock. Alone time is over."

Standing to one side, Bassinae watched as the others joked and commiserated with Cade. *It was just a friendly kiss. Something best friends share to show their affection for one another.* Then Cade's gaze focused on her with an intensity she'd didn't recognize coming from him. She touched her fingertips to her lips, and he smiled.

✳ ✳ ✳ ✳

"You can stop babying me." Vanity made Cade want to slap the long brown fingers of the woman walking beside him off his arm, but he restrained himself because he also loved the sensations her touch brought him. Still, he didn't like the implication that he was an invalid. He endured instead. After all, this was Miss Mary Sunshine, and if he removed her hand, she'd start another pep talk. He couldn't stand another happy, happy, everything's-coming-up-roses lecture.

"I don't want you to fall. So get over yourself." This statement was delivered with one of Bassinae's patented brilliant smiles.

As if. I'm not that bad off. But when she looked at him like that, he was a goner. Since the accident the sunlight that Bassinae routinely distributed in liberal doses to everyone around her had affected him in strange ways. For example, even though he'd been pissy, he couldn't stop the grin that flashed onto his face or the words that tumbled from his lips. "You know you love me when I growl."

She cocked an eyebrow at him. "I love you when you're not acting like a wounded lion better."

An ache not associated with his injury flooded his chest. Love? She loved him like a brother. During the days he'd spent in the hospital with her at his side, it had grown more and more clear to him that he didn't want her to remain in the sister category of his affections. Darcelle? Yes. She was the epitome of the bratty younger sibling out to prove she could best her big brother.

But Bassinae, she was special. She'd been there at every single one of his physical therapy sessions, helping and encouraging him, brightening his days with that brilliant smile of hers. The touch of her hands on his body had been glorious, even when she'd worked on painfully cramped muscles. He'd found himself hanging on to her for support whether he needed to or not.

She was damn pretty. Not an ounce of fat on her dancer's body. And stamina. She could compete with anyone from his military unit on endurance, both physical and emotional. She'd been through hell and back, yet she was a bundle of encouragement and positive thinking. All true before the accident, before near death had clarified matters for him. She'd said she felt like she needed something more in her life. Fuck if he didn't too. Her.

And here she was once again devoting her spare time to getting him back on his feet. Something he needed to happen yesterday instead of sometime in the future.

His chance to truly be there for Sebastian had come, and he was out of the fight. But not for long. If he knew one thing about Bassinae, she would drive him hard enough to gain ground without overdoing and relapsing. She'd been his friend ever since he'd arrived emotionally battered to take up the post of Sebastian's personal bodyguard. A job that had seemed more make-work than real until Sebastian brought him in on his criminal activities. If someone was aiming for Sebastian, the need for security now became paramount. And here he was, scuffing his way down the hall that his apartment opened onto.

"Have they figured out who was behind the accident?"

Bassinae scowled. "No. Max looked into the trucking company and the individuals responsible for maintaining and operating the truck, but he found no clear connections to Sebastian. The CEO himself apologized and is running his own internal investigation and cooperating with the police. But it looks like they're going to rule it an accident. For now, Sebastian is waiting to see if someone tries again before standing down the extra security."

"Fuck." He brushed a hand through his hair.

Bassinae gave him a pinch. "Language, bub."

"Ow!" He flinched away from her.

"Sorry. Didn't mean to hurt the poor pussy cat." She giggled, taking the sting out of the taunt. "When we get back to your place, you need a shower. And then maybe I can do something about that shaggy mane of yours. I don't think I've ever seen it this long."

He allowed her attempt to distract him to succeed. "You like it longer?" His dark blonde curls fell in a cascade around his shoulders when he shook them out and eyed her.

She studied him. "You could pull it into a man bun now. Are you keeping the beard?"

They reached the end of the corridor and turned. Rubbing his fingers over his chin, he shrugged. "I don't know. Does it look good?"

"It has potential."

"Potential?"

She grinned and prodded him with her palm to the small of his back. "Now you're grasping for compliments. Come on. Walk faster."

Cade picked up speed. "I want to hit the gym. Doc said I could start resistance training today."

"Okay, after lunch, but I expect you to spend time in the pool, too. And tomorrow, a short run. The repair nanites have healed your pelvic fracture. All we need to do is reboot your physical conditioning."

He agreed with a grunt. "Yeah. I'm with you. I have to get back up to speed. No more lying around."

Bassinae laughed. "You've only been home two days. And you haven't been lounging in front of the vidscreen." She patted his arm when he huffed his frustration. "You'll get there."

"Not soon enough." He slid his fingers along the side of his head, tangling them in his hair and yanking before dropping his arm. "Sebastian is in trouble. I need to have his back."

She pulled to a halt and blocked his way, gripping his elbow. "Stop worrying. Security has been increased in the building, and Max is accompanying Sebastian everywhere, along with another guard as the driver."

His eyes closed, Cade heaved a sigh. "I know." He lifted his eyelids to find her deep brown gaze searching his face. "I know. But it's my job, and I owe Sebastian."

The next instant he was engulfed in her tight embrace. "You're a good man, Cade Johnson, but you're not a superhero. Sebastian will be fine until you're ready to resume your duties."

Fuck. His heart seemed to shift, and then it accelerated, drumming a faster beat that matched the heat speeding through his body. The press of the soft mounds of her breasts against his chest, the light scent of the oil she used on her hair, and the suppleness of her frame beneath his palms, all combined to ignite a heady desire to fuse himself to her, to make her his. But this was Bassinae. He peeled himself from her grasp, looking away, hoping to the gods she hadn't noticed his burgeoning arousal, and muttered, "Yeah."

She patted his arm. "Come on."

He glanced sideways, trying to determine if she'd detected his far from brotherly reaction to her hug. But she seemed unfazed. Good. If he wanted to be with Bassinae, he'd have to find a way through the wall she'd erected around her life. He'd learned early on that she

21

didn't engage in casual sex, and she never intended to become involved with a man again. Ever.

That hadn't been a problem until the accident. Maybe he'd knocked a screw loose, because the woman he'd always seen as a friend, had now been placed on his list for something more. Not that he'd actually had a list. When he'd joined Sebastian's crew, he hadn't been in a mood to take up romantically with any woman, let alone Bassinae. Yeah, when he'd first been introduced to her, he had wanted to explore every inch of her body, make her lose control, and discover what expression she wore when he brought her to climax. But he'd leashed that beast. He'd been warned. Bassinae had been badly hurt, and he didn't add to any woman's pain. As their friendship grew, he'd stopped thinking of her in that way.

But now... everything had changed. Being with her was the highlight of these long, tedious days of recovery. She was the first woman he'd ever been able to relax completely with. She accepted him, believed in him, and made him feel like the man he was before that last horrendous week on Undoa Prime.

He didn't want to have sex with her. No, he wanted to make love to her. And that was different. She wasn't a slot B for his tab A. If he could, he would ensure that her life was filled with goodness and joy, protecting her, standing by her, and... *Fuck!* He clenched the hair on the top of his head with his fist. No way was he going to use the l-word. Not even think it. Whatever he was feeling, he had to keep it from Bassinae until he figured out how to induce the stubborn female to recognize that he wasn't like her former boyfriend. That men weren't naturally given to abusing their girlfriends. That a Special Forces commando trained to kill, maim, and destroy would never, ever harm the woman he loved.

"Buck up. Things aren't that bad." She grabbed his hand and pulled him into his apartment, shoving him toward the bathroom. "Now go get clean. You're getting aromatic, and I don't want to smell you while I trim your hair."

The twitch her ass made when she walked away from him brought his cock back to full attention. He groaned, stepped inside, closed the door behind him, and leaned against it, knocking his head against the wood. How the hell was he going to be around Bassinae sporting a nonstop erection? He'd dropped weight, so his pants were roomier, but with a cock the size of his they might not be big enough to hide the true nature of his affection for her. If not, he'd have to invest in something baggy. Meanwhile, there was one certain way of taming a hard-on.

He set the shower to hot, stripped, and climbed under the pelting water. The massage setting of the showerhead was his favorite, but he switched to soft rain. A hand planted on the cool tile above his head, he leaned into the spray, letting it soak his hair and drizzle heat down his back. He sighed, wanting Bassinae so bad he could almost taste her. But until he did, he would never experience the flavor of sunshine. Or the sensation of her gliding around his cock while he whispered dirty words in her ear.

Fuck all. The dispenser plopped a generous dollop of soap into his hand. After smearing it over his erection, he fisted it, pulling in long strokes from root to tip. A manly pine-forest scent wafted up to his nose, nothing like the flowery aroma that trailed after Bassinae. His Bassinae. The woman he needed beyond anything, needed to strip, to explore with his mouth and teeth, and to discover all the shades of brown that colored her delectable skin. She would open to him, tender and responsive. The heat generated by their give-and-take would fuse them, make them one, and he would find the home he'd always longed for, hidden in the depths of her heart.

"Bassinae." Her name slipped from his lips, part worship, part plea. Lightning speared through him, bursting through his balls and up his cock. A strangled cry ripped from his throat. His cum spattered the shower wall to drip in milky tears under the gentle fall of water. Physically he was sated, but that other ache, the longing, hadn't subsided with his release. *What the hell am I going to do?*

CHAPTER TWO

BASSINAE WALKED ALONG the side of the Caribbean blue pool. Light played across the water from the floor-to-ceiling windows that lined one wall of the room. The near end held white tables and chairs, while chaise lounges formed a line along where the sun streamed in. Longer than it was wide, the pool was primarily used for swimming laps, which Cade now did, his strokes long and sure, powering him through the water. It would take someone who had watched him swim freestyle in the past to detect the moments when his kick went slightly out of sync with his arms. He was overcompensating for pelvic and hip muscles that had been torn. Although fully restored, they had lost strength, throwing his rhythm off.

He'd also taken a hit to his stamina, but it was returning quicker than she had expected. A man of such vigor and grace was a pleasure to watch. Cade knew he was good-looking. Enough so that he didn't strut or preen like some men. He and Sebastian were similar in that respect. Both resembled untamed wildcats, but where Sebastian was a black panther, reeking of danger, a hunter stalking its prey, Cade was a lion. And not just because his long golden hair reminded her of a mane. The predator in him wasn't as obviously on display. He could lounge, fully relaxed, taking in his surroundings with regal indifference, batting at a cub that got too rambunctious while sunning himself. An image of Darcelle challenging Cade flashed through her mind, and she chuckled. But potent ability was always there, rippling through his muscled body, ready for when he leaped into action to protect those he considered part of his pride.

When he reached the end of the pool, he made a smooth underwater turn and headed back the way he'd come. He was pushing himself. This was the second lap he'd taken beyond what she'd asked him to do. She had to monitor him to keep him from overdoing. "This is the last lap. I want you out of that pool."

He waved a finger at her with his next stroke to acknowledge her demand. At the wall, he treaded water and hollered, "I could handle a few more laps."

"Cade Johnson, get your ass out of there now. And no back talk." She strode to the ladder, hands on hips covered in light blue athletic shorts, and glared at him as he climbed out.

He grinned at her. "Yes, ma'am." He shook his head, and water scattered in an arc around him.

"Hey!" She jumped away, laughing. "Careful or I'll dose you with my herbal tincture."

"Oh gods. Not that stuff." He smoothed his dripping curls from his forehead with both hands. "My hair started falling out the time you made me drink that awful crap."

Side by side they walked to where a pile of sea-green towels was stacked on a table. "It did not. You're making that up because you don't like the taste."

He grabbed one and scrubbed his head, eliminating the moisture that was dribbling onto his well-developed chest. "Who in their right mind would like the taste?"

"It's not that bad."

Rather than respond, he stopped rubbing the towel on his legs and brought his gaze up to look at her, allowing his expression to reveal he thought she was nuts.

She swatted his upper arm. "Oh, go rinse off and change. I'll meet you in the massage room."

His gaze focused on toweling his feet, he muttered, "Yeah, I don't think I need one today."

"That's not for you to decide. Who has a massage therapy license here?"

The towel bunched in his hand, he looked perturbed.

Why the hell is he saying no to a massage? He usually begs for them. *"You have something you're hiding from me."*

His eyes widened for an instant. "No. Nothing. I didn't want to keep you any more than I already have. You've been awesome, but surely you have your own stuff do."

She assumed the dramatic expression of an overburdened martyr. "You are a difficult man to train, but someone has to make sure you get back on your feet. You'd be knotted like a pretzel if I didn't take care of you. Which means a massage, buddy."

The grin he flashed at her wasn't in the least sympathetic. Her natural response was to return it with a smile of her own, but when she did, a look came into his eyes, a glint of something she wasn't used to seeing. Was that desire?

"All right. I won't be but a minute," he said and strolled off to the dressing room.

She bit her lip and watched him. His swim trunks did little to hide the athletic perfection of his body. He was above average in height by a couple of inches. He was muscular, but not in the way a weight lifter might be, and what he had was well honed. Enough to make most ladies drool. Every part of him was finely tuned, under his complete control. He was the fantasy many women desired for a lover. That gorgeous ass alone put him leaps and bounds ahead of most men. No, she must have been mistaken. Cade saw her as a friend, which was what she wanted. It was a miracle she had a close male friend at all. Before Cade, she would have said it was impossible.

She shook her head, pushing those thoughts aside, and left the pool to walk to the massage room down the hall. Once she arrived, she set up the table with clean sheets, put on relaxing music, and set her favorite oil in the warmer. She loved this space, with its muted blues and greens. An abstract piece of art made from tiny square tiles in all the shades of a warm sea hung, filling most of one wall. She stood and switched the music to ocean sounds. That was better.

Heels perched on the second rung, she sat on the stool in the room to wait, propping her elbows on her knees and her chin in her hands. She rubbed a finger over the ashy skin of her knee, reminding herself to buy more shea butter. Her mind returned to thoughts of

Cade, but rather than evaluating his progress or making plans for future sessions, she again contemplated that glint in his eyes.

What if he is starting to see me as more than a friend? Would that mean an end to the camaraderie we share? Early on he'd hit on her, once. She'd put a stop to that with a firm, polite refusal, which he'd honored ever since. Their friendship had flourished with sex off the table. And that's all he'd wanted back then, sex. She'd told him a little of what she'd been through, and that she never imagined herself getting involved with a man again.

Oddly, becoming intimate wasn't immediately as repulsive as it had been in the past. Not, at least, if the man were Cade. But even as she contemplated the prospect, her stomach began to churn and ice crystals began forming in her blood, freezing her from the inside out. It was this reaction that settled the matter. Fear would always hold her back. Her counselor had said it didn't have to be that way, that she could work through the psychological block, but she had to want to. So far she hadn't found a reason to go through the turmoil dealing with her past would create.

"How's the water deep in that well?"

She popped her head up and frowned at Cade. "What?"

Cade waved a hand at her and dropped the boots and socks he'd been carrying on the floor. "Never mind. You looked deep in thought."

"Deep in the well. Deep in thought," he said when her expression didn't change.

"Oh. Uh. Nothing important." She slipped off the stool and headed toward the door. "I'll let you get ready."

He was already pulling his shirt over his head, so his response was muffled. "You don't have to leave." He threw the garment onto the chair standing against one wall and unbuttoned his pants. The nonchalance he affected was a little stiff.

"Fine." Tension snaked through her. "I'll get the oil ready." She spun away from him, fiddling with the bottle longer than necessary until the sound of him climbing on the table and settling under the top sheet stopped. She blew out a deep breath and turned, briskly smoothing the sheet over him and folding it back to bare his chest. He always wanted her to start on his shoulders after a swim.

"You looked in great shape out there." She smoothed her hands over his skin, searching for any place he was tight or where knots had formed.

"My rhythm's off. I lost muscle mass in that left hip. The swim did me good though. I can feel it here." Under the sheet his hand rubbed the left side of his pelvis.

"I'll put a speed-heal patch on it later. Be sure you're drinking plenty of water."

He grunted. "I am."

Silence fell, and she drifted into that zen state where her mind and physical being no longer seemed separate parts of who she was but one fused whole, at peace within herself and with the world. It's what she enjoyed about massage. Not only did her client benefit, but she was also invigorated by the self-expression through touch.

Cade's body was a pleasure to work on. He was in his prime, physically healthy, but also more aware than most of how each part of him worked and what was needed to keep himself in top shape. And he loved to be touched. It wasn't unusual for him to show up at her door and plead for her to give him a massage. She moved around him, sliding the sheet aside to do each of his legs.

When her fingers found their way to his pelvis, he surged up from the table, pulling the sheet up. "My back needs attention." He gave his right shoulder a brief rub and flipped over.

Her initial response was to take a step back. "Okay." For all the world he looked like he was trying to hide behind the sheet. When he turned over, she noticed a bulge under it. It had happened before. A cock stand was a side effect that could happen to men during a massage, which was why she didn't have male clients. A small part of the reason, at least. That they were men being the primary cause. After the first time with Cade, he had never been embarrassed about it, making stupid jokes instead. He made no lame comments this time. If he wanted to ignore it, she would too. She shook her hands out and then she resettled the sheet over his lower half and went to work on his upper back. His fingers were clamped on the edge of the massage table. "Are you okay?"

"Uh, sure. I felt a twinge and thought you should get on it."

Bassinae continued searching for the spot that was bothering him. "Hmmm. I'm not feeling any knots."

"Pooh. Yeah. Right there. That's where it hurts."

She put effort into soothing the area, shaking her head. Something had definitely changed. Cade was obviously trying to hide his reaction to her. Which must mean he didn't want this any more than she did. If she ignored the problem, it should go away. Treat Cade as she always had, and things would get back to normal once he was fully recovered from the accident. He was stressed out and probably confusing a need for physical reassurance with romantic notions. Everything would work out fine. It had to, because she didn't want to lose her best friend.

* * * *

"Bassinae. Bassinae, dear."

Bassinae, seated behind the front desk at Do It Now, lifted her gaze from the vidscreen where she'd been inputting her class schedule for the next month. Streaming toward her like a naval space carrier, wrapped in a sapphire-blue spring coat, her ebony hair pinned in a perfect French twist, Adele St. Croix waved her palm in the air.

What is Sebastian's mother doing here? Although she was a benefactor of Do It Now and a member of its board, she didn't enmesh herself in its daily running. Bassinae stood. "Ma'am."

"Oh, none of that." She continued waving her hand. "Call me Adele. I'm here on a personal matter."

Behind her a woman wearing an equally expensive designer coat waited, clasping and unclasping her hands. Dark circles underscored the woman's pain-filled and worried eyes. Adele drew her forward. "Let me introduce you. Bassinae, I'd like you to meet a very good friend of mine, Georgia Bernard. Georgia, this is Bassinae; she's a colleague of my son's and also works here at Do It Now." Adele returned her gaze to Bassinae and asked, "Can we use one of the counseling rooms for a moment?"

"Certainly, ma'am." Bassinae corrected herself when Sebastian's mother tipped her head at her and gave her a very sophisticated stink eye. "Adele. Right this way." Once the women were settled in chairs, Bassinae asked, "Can I get you anything?"

"No, no, dear. We've been here for a while and have been plied with refreshments at every turn." Adele gazed at Georgia, her expression full of compassion. "I finally convinced Georgia to leave that ogre she married. Do It Now will assist her as it has so many other unfortunate women with the ramifications of escaping an abusive relationship, but"—Adele returned her focus to Bassinae—"she has another matter that is rather outside the purview of Do It Now. I believe Sebastian is the proper person to assist her, but I'm not supposed to know anything about that. I'd like to maintain that fiction. It occurred to me that this problem might come to you through your work here at Do It Now, and you could pass it on to my son."

Bassinae smiled gently. "I see. So what is it you think Sebastian can do to help?"

Head lifted high, Adele said, "Now dear, you are wonderfully discreet, but I know all about Sebastian's illicit activities in the pursuit of justice. How could I not? Jeanne is my daughter. After Cheyenne's rescue, she told me everything. In strictest confidence."

Bassinae snapped her mouth closed when she realized her jaw had dropped. This was one bombshell she didn't want to go off while she was in the vicinity of Sebastian. "Okay."

Bassinae turned to Georgia Bernard, a timid mouse compared to Adele, and waited for the woman to meet her eyes before saying, "Ms. Bernard...Georgia, what can I do for you."

It was as though Bassinae had thrown her a lifeline and Georgia had snatched onto it. She edged forward in her chair, her face a mixture of anxiety and determination. *Maybe not so timid.*

"I'm not worried about how divorce will affect me financially. The wonderful people here have assured me they will do whatever is necessary to obtain an equitable arrangement." She paused for a moment and placed her fists on top of the table between them. "But Hugo has something I must get back. A set of heirloom jewelry from my mother's side of my family. Hugo told me he sold it, but I'm certain he didn't. It's locked inside his office safe. He always threatened to sell the jewelry. Held it over my head for years until recently when he claimed he'd engaged Tajan to sell it privately, but I'd know if he had. It would make a splash. Even were the sale private, rumors would have leaked." Adele's face hardened. "I want that jewelry back. It doesn't belong to him. It's mine."

Bassinae reached out a hand to cover one of Adele's clenched fists. "You've come to the right person. If anyone can recover your jewelry, it's Sebastian. Let me talk to him first, and then we can arrange a meeting. He'll have questions for you."

"You really think he can?" Georgia's gaze darted from Bassinae to Adele, who gave her a firm nod, and then to her fists on the table. She thumped them down, straightened her shoulders, and said, "Good. Let's do it."

After she saw the ladies out, Bassinae commed Sebastian's primary assistant to arrange an appointment, only to discover he was working from home that day. If she hurried, she could catch him before he left with Darcelle to attend an exhibition at the Musée Fédéral d'Art. So she trotted to the elevator, acknowledging the guard stationed there, and went straight up to the penthouse, messaging Max that she was on the way.

He met her at the apartment's front door. At first glance you'd believe he was the same calm, cool, collected man who kept Sebastian's life running smoothly. On closer inspection Bassinae saw the slightly wrinkled brow. Max was troubled, and if Max was, then there was something to be worried about.

"Morning, Bassinae. What's up?"

"Someone came to me at Do It Now with a problem that should interest Sebastian, but maybe now isn't a good time for another job."

"Let him be the judge of that. I told him you were coming. He's waiting in his office."

31

Sebastian's door was open, and he waved them in when they stopped at the threshold. "You should stay," Bassinae said to Max. He joined her in the navy upholstered armchairs opposite the sleek walnut desk that dominated the room. Sebastian sat leaning back in the desk chair he'd had built to his specifications, also in a deep blue color.

"Max said you had something you needed to share with me. Is everything all right with Cade?" Sebastian asked Bassinae.

"Cade is doing very well. He should be back to work within the week."

"That's good to hear. I was concerned he might push too hard and set himself back."

Smiling broadly, Bassinae shook her head. "He probably would, but I've been watching him like a hawk. He was in the pool today, and although his left hip was giving him some trouble, he could still outswim most men."

"That man is one of the most fit bastards on this planet," Sebastian said, a wry grin crossing his face.

At the image of Cade walking to the locker room in his swim trunks, sleek muscles moving under golden-brown skin, a tinge of heat flushed Bassinae's cheeks. Disconcerted that she'd been thinking of Cade in those terms, let alone in front of Sebastian and Max, she tightened her lips.

"Keeps us all on our toes," Max said.

His full attention on Bassinae, Sebastian asked, "If not Cade, what did you want to discuss?"

Bassinae swallowed, grateful the discussion had turned from Cade to the topic that had brought her here. "A woman came to Do It Now today. I should stop and say that she is a friend of your mother."

"My mother?" Sebastian's voice was wary.

"Yes. Georgia Bernard."

"Ah. Yes. She is one of my mother's oldest and dearest friends. I take it Georgia has finally left her husband." He crossed his arms.

"She has." Bassinae bobbed her head. "Your mother accompanied her to Do It Now."

Sebastian grunted. "Of course she did. She's been urging Georgia to take this step for years. I don't know what pushed her to kick that disgusting asswipe to the curb, but it's high time she did. He's been verbally, emotionally, and psychologically abusing her. Never physical as far as I've heard, but I think that's because he knows someone would step in. But I don't see what I can do to help Georgia. Do It Now has the staff and advisers on retainer that should be able to handle anything Hugo throws at her."

"And they are taking superb care of Ms. Bernard..." Bassinae paused, clasping her hands in her lap and steeling herself to maintain eye contact with Sebastian. "But I overheard her discussing what she claimed was her greatest fear with your mother."

Lying didn't come easily to Bassinae. She bit her lip, tempted to confess his mother's secret. But the urge was short-lived. After all, it was such a small omission, and he and his mother would both be happier if he didn't discover that his illegal activities had been revealed. So she continued without disclosing that tidbit. Perhaps she could get Adele St. Croix to make the admission herself.

"Which is?"

Sebastian has to sense I'm holding something back. He has that look in his eye. Oh gods, just do what you came to do. "Ms. Bernard believes that Mr. Bernard has kept an heirloom jewelry set that he claims to have sold. The set has been handed down in her family for many generations. It's very important to her. He told her he sold the jewelry, but she's certain he said that to hurt her and that it's still in his safe, one she has no access to, so she's never been able to confirm her suspicion." Bassinae was proud that she didn't flinch when Sebastian's eyebrows knit together.

"So you stepped in and told her you were acquainted with someone who could help with the problem?"

She went ramrod straight. "I did. I explained that you would want to meet with her to get all the details."

Sebastian scowled, his voice a low rumble. "You didn't give her my name, did you? In front of my mother?"

"No." Bassinae held her hands up. "I would never reveal to your mother that you're a cat burglar." That was true. She hadn't spilled the beans. Adele St. Croix had discovered what her son was doing without a word from Bassinae. Adele's flamboyant personality may make some doubt her intellect, but Bassinae recognized that she was one savvy woman. It would have been only a matter of time, with the right facts in hand, until she put two and two together without Jeanne's help at all.

His eyes hard, Sebastian said, "Good." He raised his steepled fingers to tap against his mouth. "I don't see how I can meet with Georgia. She's not capable of keeping that kind of secret from my mother." He dropped his hands and pursed his lips, his eyes focused on the ceiling.

"Perhaps someone else could conduct all necessary interviews," Max said.

"That could work." Sebastian gave Max an intense stare. "You?"

Max's serene expression didn't change. "No. Not me. I've met the woman on multiple occasions." His placid appearance never altered when he added, "I like to believe I'm memorable."

Unable to help herself, Bassinae gave a snort of amusement.

"You have me there," Sebastian said. Then his gaze riveted on her. "Bassinae could do it."

Her mouth dropped open and then snapped shut. She was doing a lot of that lately. Stomach tight, she said, "Me?"

"That's an excellent suggestion." Max draped his arm across the back of Bassinae's chair and said, "You could do it."

Are they crazy? "I couldn't possibly. I wouldn't know what to ask."

Sebastian looked entirely too pleased about the idea to Bassinae's way of thinking. "We'll work out the details before your meeting. And if I need further information, you can always speak with Georgia again."

"But..."

Sebastian clapped his hands. "It's settled."

"What's settled?" Darcelle entered the office wearing one of those floaty pastel dresses that were the current pinnacle of fashion. She perched a hip on Sebastian's desk and eyed each of them.

Sebastian rolled his chair close to her and put a hand around her waist. "Bassinae is going to do the interview for our next heist. We'll be stealing jewelry."

"Sounds like fun." She placed her fingers on his shoulder, giving the wool of his bespoke dark gray suit jacket a rub. "But now we need to get going, or we'll be late for the exhibition. You'll have to wait to play until later."

"Right you are." Sebastian stood, dropping a kiss on the top of his wife's head. "We'll work on this tomorrow." To Bassinae he said, "Bring Cade. I want to see how he's doing in person." He gave Max a questioning look. "You'll arrange it?"

"Yes, sir."

"Excellent."

Bassinae followed Max to his office to compare schedules. It's not that big of a deal. I'll get the details about what the pieces look like, their size, the location of the safe, and security measures in the house. Sebastian and Darcelle will do the hard work. *Still it was exciting. She was becoming a more integral part of the team. She couldn't help but laugh at her case of nerves.*

CHAPTER THREE

CADE WAS PULLING on his shoes when he heard the tap at his door. When he opened it, Bassinae gave him a big smile. "Ready?"

"Yeah."

He hugged the wall in the elevator, attempting to avoid the slightest contact with her, knowing it would harden the semi-erection that was his norm anytime he came near her now. It helped that she settled herself with a shoulder against the opposite side.

Upon entering the conference room, he brushed past her to reach the next seat along the table. "Excuse me." He felt her flinch forward to avoid him and frowned.

He sat, flicking a glance at her and then away. She focused all her attention on Sebastian. The fingers of Cade's right hand kept up a rhythmic tapping on his thigh that he tried unsuccessfully to quit, only to have them start again almost at once. He didn't need to be here for this. Sebastian could have handled this alone. Hell, he was handling it alone. But Bassinae said Sebastian wanted him to come, so Cade had come.

The conference room was a spare, utilitarian space with blank walls that were actually vidscreens. Bassinae and Sebastian had their heads together, sharing a vidscreen embedded in the table. He had been walking her through the questions he wanted Georgia Bernard to answer.

Bassinae was a vision in tight shorts in a color that was somewhere between orange and pink with a name he'd never remember. The stripes on her T-shirt followed her sleek curves. What he wouldn't give to slide his hands over them. He dropped his gaze, not wanting either of them to glimpse his thoughts.

"Right, if she has access to images of the jewelry, we'll want those. And any interior shots of the house. When Jeanne returns from vacation, she ought to be able to find the original architectural plans. We'll have you go over those with Georgia, but for now get a basic idea of the main entrances and Hugo's office in relation to them." Sebastian leaned back. "Don't worry. Use the outline and remember that if you leave out something important, you'll be doing follow-up anyway."

"I got this," Bassinae said, her voice bubbly.

Cade brought his gaze to her, enthralled by the effervescent delight that was Bassinae. Why he'd never realized how exquisitely beautiful she was before was beyond him. Even in a T-shirt and shorts she was the epitome of grace. Freeze her statue-still at any random moment and she'd be the perfect model for a painter or sculptor.

A smile like the ones that warmed his heart when they were directed at him flashed across her face. This time Sebastian was the beneficiary.

Sebastian responded with a half grin. "Darcelle suggested that I ask you to work up your own plan for how to recover the jewelry. She believes, and I agree, that you'd be a stronger team member if you got some training on strategic planning. You never know when you might be needed to cover for one of us or be the only person who can get a member of the team out of a sticky situation. We'll go over your suggestions when the team meets for our first planning session."

Her shoulders rose and fell as Bassinae took a deep breath and released it. "I can't tell you how grateful I am for the opportunity to learn. Thank you for believing in me."

"You're a smart woman, Bassinae. You just need more opportunities to prove it," Sebastian said.

Bassinae stood. "I'll go check on Ms. Bernard now. See if she has time to do this right away. Your mother talked her into staying at Do It Now rather than going to a hotel. I think she was worried that Ms. Bernard might change her mind and return home without someone to support her decision."

"I'm glad Georgia came to Do It Now. She's one reason my mother and I founded the shelter. Comm me to let me know when you've finished with her. Darcelle and I are staying in tonight, so we could go over it with the team then," Sebastian said.

"Will do." Bassinae raised a tentative hand to Cade. "Bye."

He grunted, and she turned and made a swift exit.

Sebastian turned his penetrating pale green gaze on Cade, who did his best not to squirm. Questions filled his boss's eyes, ones Cade would prefer not to deal with. The damn man was far too perceptive.

"Have you had a fight with Bassinae?"

"What?" Cade blinked rapidly. "No. We're fine."

Instead of responding immediately, Sebastian continued to stare at him. The instant before Cade was about to say something further, Sebastian spoke. "You're not fine. The two of you are edging around one another like a litter of startled kittens. Hair standing on end. Backs arched. The only thing you're not doing is hissing at each other, at least not in front of me."

His tone grudging, Cade said, "We're not fighting."

"I thought maybe you let your irritation at the speed of your recovery get the best of you. So, no sniping at Bassinae?" Sebastian cocked an eyebrow at him.

Cade scowled. "I would never treat Bassinae that way."

"What is it then?"

His gaze settled on the edge of the conference table, Cade winced, started to speak, and winced again. "I have feelings for her. And I think she knows." He looked up, locking his gaze on Sebastian's. "I don't know what to do about it."

Sebastian crossed his arms over his chest. "That's simple. Talk to her."

Lips pressed tight, Cade sighed. "I can't. Acknowledging how I... It will screw up everything. She made it clear a long time ago that she doesn't want a relationship with a man. Ever."

"People change their minds."

Cade ran a hand through his hair, staring at but not seeing the far wall. "But if she doesn't, I could lose her as a friend. I'd rather have her in my life than not at all."

"The way you're going, you could lose her anyway. If Bassinae's the one, you don't want to let the opportunity to be with her slip through your fingers because you're afraid of your friendship turning sour. Maybe you should try some old-fashioned wooing."

The suggestion didn't lighten the heavy load that weighed on him. If anything, it added to the burden. But Sebastian was right. Doing nothing was making things worse. If he told her, put the truth out on the table, that he wanted their friendship to be something more, she might push him away. She needed to figure out for herself that a man—no, that *he* could be trusted with her heart.

"Woo her, huh?" Was he serious? Cade glanced at Sebastian, who shrugged his right shoulder.

"If your feelings have changed, how you treat her should too." His voice grew firmer. "Whatever you do, don't try to jump her bones."

Cade's jaw tightened. "I know that. I'm not an idiot. She'd bloody my nose and properly so." He brought his knuckle to his lips. "Candy? Flowers? That kind of thing?"

Sebastian snorted and shook his head. "You may not be an idiot, but you're damn close. Do you think candy and flowers would have any effect on Bassinae?"

"No. Probably not. But who knows with women?"

Sebastian gave him a half smile. "That's for sure. Bassinae isn't into material possessions, but she will notice if you do things for her. Something you wouldn't normally do. What would she appreciate? Think about it. You can't go wrong spending quality time with a woman and making sure her every need is met. And compliments. Not just about how she looks, but how she makes you feel. What she's done that's special. She'll see you in a whole new light. I guarantee it."

Eyebrows scrunched, Cade asked, "How'd you get to know so much about women?"

Rubbing a hand along his jaw, Sebastian chuckled. "Have you met my wife? Darcelle isn't bashful about telling me exactly what she wants and lecturing me on how to treat a woman you're supposed to love. I try never to forget the lessons she's taught me. Darcelle's remedial training is never fun."

Cade could well imagine. He'd been on the receiving end of one of Darcelle's tongue lashings more than once. A verbal correction from her was bad enough, but Cade was certain she used every weapon in her arsenal when Sebastian pissed her off. The pair might go at each other hammer and tongs, but when the tumult quieted, they were like lovebirds, billing and cooing. Then you evaded their company for completely different reasons from when they were fighting.

"Better you than me." Cade shook his head.

Sebastian grinned, fingering the edge of the conference table. "You ready to come back to work? Bassinae says you are."

"Did she? She didn't tell me that. Yeah. I mean, I enjoy working out, but that's all I've been doing. I'm bored out of my mind."

Sebastian smirked. "Can't have you lovesick and bored out of your mind at the same time."

Cade narrowed his eyes and feigned an irritated grunt.

"Tell Max you're officially back on the schedule." Then Sebastian stood and slapped Cade on the back. "You'll figure it out. Men have been in your position for centuries, and somehow the women keep taking us on."

Cade slumped with one elbow on the table and his chin on his fist. "Yeah." He ignored Sebastian's chuckle as his boss left the room. *But what do I do if the woman won't change her mind?*

* * * *

The effect of a good night's rest was striking on Georgia Bernard's face. The dark circles, though still present, had faded, and her skin tone wasn't as sallow. Bassinae had suggested they go to her apartment where they could talk on the terrace. Once they were settled, each with a cup, she asked Georgia about her impressions of Do It Now.

"I've been amazed at the kindness shown to me. Adele has always spoken of the support they offer to women..." She clasped the pearl pendant that hung from her neck. "I should have come sooner. The embarrassment of revealing my private life to strangers held me back. How could they care about a woman whose own husband scorned her? Hugo had me convinced I was worthless. That I couldn't make it in the world without him. Better the devil you know. That's what I told myself. He never physically harmed me. I believed what he said about me. That it was something inside me, my fault that he treated me the way he did." A sad smile crossed her face. "I was wrong, and the people at Do It Now are helping me see that and to stand on my own."

It frustrated Bassinae that abuse victims assumed they had nothing to complain of because they hadn't been hit. But she understood the mentality. She hadn't run from her own situation until Jessil had broken her jaw, even though he'd been slapping her around for months. After that incident she had refused to return to him when she was released from the hospital with no money and only the clothes on her back. She'd been so hungry she'd taken to panhandling. That's when, thank the gods, she met Sebastian. Georgia had nothing to be ashamed about.

Bassinae covered Georgia's hand with her own. "I've been there. I was in an abusive relationship too."

A look of pained concern formed on Georgia's face. "I'm so sorry."

How could anyone abuse this sweet woman? Bassinae smiled softly and patted Georgia's hand. "Good came of it. Sebastian saw me begging outside a business he owned, and rather than call the police, he took me inside and demanded I tell him my story. With his support I turned my life around and became part of Do It Now from the very start. You'll be joining one of my exercise classes soon. We help women wherever they're at. For some that means addictions. For others it means helping them care for their children. Each woman's story is unique, but the answer for all is to develop a healthy mind, body, and spirit." After taking a sip of tea, Bassinae continued. "But we have another important topic to discuss: your jewelry. If it's okay, I'm going to record our conversation."

"That would be fine." Georgia clasped her hands and held them in her lap.

Bassinae held up one finger. "Before I do, I want to remind you not to use Sebastian's name. He doesn't want you to know he's the one helping you. That's why I'm interviewing you. I'll call him the team leader."

"Yes." Georgia nodded. "Team leader. I'll remember."

Bassinae placed her handheld tablet between them and set it to audio logging. "Ms. Bernard, I need to ask you about the jewelry and then some questions that will help our team leader develop a plan to retrieve the set for you. First we need a description of the jewels."

"Of course. It's a full parure, a set, including a necklace, bracelet, brooch, and earrings. All were designed in the twenty-first century by Alessandro Castellani." Georgia leaned forward, a glow in her eyes as she spoke of her heirlooms. "It was a commission to create a modern version of a necklace found in Pharaoh Tutankhamun's tomb, the pectoral of Kheper scarab. It's a replica made of gold inlaid with semiprecious gemstones. That design was then copied for the other pieces."

"It must be worth a great deal."

"Yes. But how much is hard to determine. I think the last time it was valued for insurance purposes, it was 2.3 million credits."

It was difficult for Bassinae to imagine having jewelry that cost that much. Living and working in the St. Croix high-rise had brought her in contact with wealth, but Sebastian and Darcelle weren't flashy people. Understated elegance and refinement was more their style. Unless you counted the areas of the penthouse where they held parties. They had been decorated with great flamboyance by Sebastian's mother, including an Egyptian foyer. Bassinae had made her way through it and the hall of sculptures many times.

"Do you have pictures of the pieces?"

"Yes. I can get them to you." Georgia drew on the tabletop with her fingers. "Each one has a winged lapis scarab with a carnelian sun disk at the top and a turquoise bowl on the bottom. The wings are lapis, turquoise, and carnelian. Very tiny inlay. The work is quite exquisite."

Bassinae smiled. "It sounds like it."

Georgia tapped her forefinger. "I want the jewelry back. It has been handed down to the oldest female in each generation of my family for centuries now. Hugo said he sold it. But I don't think you could keep something like that quiet. Rumors would be floating among collectors. So he still has it." She gripped her pendant again. "He has to."

In the past, helping Sebastian with his heists had been fun. Bassinae had always played a secondary role, often as a distraction, so one or more of the others could do something surreptitious. But this time around, on this job, her sense of purpose was greater. Sebastian had asked her to come up with her own plan for how to retrieve the pieces for Georgia. Strategic planning, he had called it. She felt more invested in this project than any of the others she'd participated in, except for when they'd snatched Jeanne's daughter, Cheyenne, from the cretin who had fathered the girl.

This felt like her mission. She'd been the one to bring it to Sebastian's attention, and it was linked to her work at Do It Now. Yeah, it was her job to help the abused women who became her clients, but she'd always thought of her work as a vocation. Her muscles tightened as she recognized that whatever it took, she would help get that jewelry back. She had nothing of her own mother's, let alone a centuries-old family heirloom. But Georgia did. If it was possible, they would do this for her. No one should have to live life with a pig like Hugo Bernard and have her greatest treasure stolen as well.

Determination filling her voice, Bassinae said, "If it's in your home, we will find it and retrieve it for you. You've asked the right people for help. The team leader and his second are both masters at cracking safes. Gaining entry without being discovered or monitored by security measures will be the tricky part. But the plan they develop will cover all that. They've recovered stolen artwork under much more difficult conditions."

Georgia's eyes widened, and she threw her hands up. "It seems a little incredible that Sebastian does this kind of thing. I would never have guessed."

"He relies on that."

Georgia covered her mouth with a hand. "Oops. I said his name."

Bassinae giggled. "Not to worry. I know how hard secrets are to keep. I'll delete that bit and start recording again." She fiddled with her tablet and said, "We're back on now," tapping to re-engage the audio recording when she said *now*.

"Do you need more tea before we go over the layout of the house?" Bassinae pointed to Georgia's cup.

"Yes, dear. That would be lovely." Bassinae poured each of them another cup while Georgia continued. "I don't know how you're going to get into the house. Hugo installed very tight security measures. I never quite understood why he felt the need, but he upgraded five years ago. It wasn't like he kept anything of irreplaceable value in the safe. Well...until now with my Egyptian set. All my expensive jewelry was kept in the vault of our bank. I wore fakes to parties and galas. Hugo said no one could tell the difference." Georgia lifted her cup to take a sip of tea.

Bassinae shook her head. "Your husband is a piece of work."

Her hand paused in midair, Georgia blinked. "He really is a frightful human being. I'm only now beginning to understand how he manipulated me, controlling every aspect of my life."

"Thankfully that is over. You needn't worry about how the team will get your jewelry back. They'll figure it out."

The clink of china on the tabletop punctuated Georgia's next statement. "I should have listened to Adele years ago."

Chapter Four

JEANNE WAS ALREADY seated in her favorite spot in the conference room, tapping away on the portable keypad she preferred to use when interfacing with the vidscreens embedded in the table. She glanced up when Bassinae slid in next to her. "Hey. Have you and Darcelle kept the men in line while I've been gone? I heard Cade got his ass handed to him by a dump truck. Haven't seen him since I got back. You get him worked into shape again?"

The smile that had initially flashed onto Bassinae's face dimmed. "He's fine. Returned to work. Max and Sebastian still haven't decided whether someone was targeting Sebastian with that accident or if it was programming failure like the trucking firm insists. For now one of the Do It Now security guards is driving Sebastian, and Cade is serving as pure bodyguard."

"Yeah. I suppose it's possible that someone has taken a dislike to Sebastian. Happens all the time. But to the point of murder? I find that hard to believe. How about you? Anything new with you?" Jeanne stilled her fingers and intently focused her gaze on Bassinae.

A soft smile spread slowly on Bassinae's lips. "I'm the go-between with the client for this op. Sebastian also asked me to come up with my own plan for how we can break in and steal the jewels. I have a few ideas from talking with Georgia. It makes me feel a bigger part of the team. Not just a minor player. You know?"

"If Sebastian thinks you can handle it, then you can."

"Well..." Bassinae gave Jeanne a rueful look. "It's a little more involved than that. You told your mother about what Sebastian did for you, so she thought he could help Georgia Bernard the same way. But your mom doesn't want him to suspect that she knows what he's up to."

Jeanne put a hand to the top of her head. "Oh gods. I should never have done that. I was such an emotional wreck back then."

"Yeah, well, I haven't shared that detail with Sebastian. He thinks that I suggested the possibility to Ms. Bernard when I met her at Do It Now and she shared her problem with me. He doesn't want Georgia to know who's helping her because she might tell your mother and let the cat out of the bag."

Jeanne snorted. "Cat burglar out of the bag. Sorry, Cheyenne's big into jokes, riddles, and puns right now."

"So how was your trip? Did you two have fun mother/daughter bonding on your island retreat?"

Her face brightening, Jeanne said, "We had a terrific time. Cheyenne ran me ragged scuba diving, water skiing, and swimming with the flutter fish. I had to demand a down day to lie on the beach and sunbathe."

Sebastian and Darcelle walked into the room, followed by Max and Cade. They seated themselves, Sebastian looking a little tired despite the impeccable bespoke suit he wore for business. Shadows smudged the skin beneath his pale green eyes. He had a lot on his plate. Maybe he should take a vacation like Jeanne. Darcelle looked as fierce and snappy as usual, even in mint green yoga pants and a tee. Sebastian sat at the head of the table with Darcelle next to him. The pair put their heads together for a private conversation. Max went to the far end, and Cade seated himself opposite Bassinae, giving a nudge to her foot with the toe of his boot and a half smile before focusing his attention on Jeanne. "Hey, lazy girl. All that sun didn't fry your brains as well as turn you golden brown, did it? If I didn't know better, I'd think you were turning yourself into a female version of me." He tossed his head, letting his tawny curls dance on top of his broad shoulders. "You growing your hair out, too?"

Deadpan, Jeanne said, "Listen, stud, if I wanted to look like anyone, it wouldn't be you. It's getting cut and dyed green soon."

"Green, huh?"

Unaffected by the teasing grin on Cade's face, Jeanne said, "Cheyenne picked the color."

Sebastian pulled his head away from Darcelle's with a leer on his face he quickly disguised when she cocked an eyebrow at him. Then he turned his attention to the others, wrapping a knuckle on the table, aiming his words at Cade and Jeanne. "If the two of you could get your mind out of the beauty salon, we have business to conduct."

Easing back into his chair, Cade let the smirk remain on his face, his gaze settled on Jeanne. She flashed a rude gesture at him and then turned her attention to Sebastian.

It was a typical interaction between Cade and the women he called friends. For whatever reason he goaded them. You couldn't say it was his competitive nature. Maybe it was. He didn't compete with Sebastian or Max. But he routinely taunted Darcelle and Jeanne, pointing out they had yet to reach his level of perfection. The pair gave him the brat right back.

But he doesn't do that with me. He doesn't play with me like that. She contemplated him. *Why? It's always been different between us. Does he assume I'm too fragile, that he'll crush me if he pokes fun at me?* A knot formed in her stomach. Was that how she wanted him to perceive her, as a victim, in need of coddling? She'd taken control of her life, yes, with the help of others, but that assistance would have been meaningless if she hadn't done the hard work of becoming a new person. Fitness trainer, massage therapist, and now a stepped-up roll with Sebastian—all were aspects of a woman no longer dependent on a man for her sense of meaning or purpose.

"Bassinae?"

The realization that she had tuned out Sebastian sent a rush of color to her cheeks. "Sorry. What did you say?"

A slight glimmer of irritation flickered in Sebastian's eyes. "The original plans for the Bernard mansion are on your vidscreen. In your conversation with Georgia, did she describe any alterations to the building?"

A little flustered, Bassinae leaned forward. "Yes. She said that five years ago an additional panic room had been added that could only be accessed via her husband's office. The room next to the office was upgraded and sealed off from the rest of the house. A new, larger safe was installed in the panic room."

Staring at the wall vidscreen where Jeanne had displayed the plans, Sebastian asked, "Did she give you the access information for the room and the safe?"

Her lips pressed into a line, Bassinae shook her head. "She didn't. Her husband's office was strictly off limits to her, so he claimed she'd never need to know how to enter that panic room. If necessary, she was to hide in the one located off her bedroom suite."

Sebastian grimaced. "Jeanne, do more digging on the contractors for that installation. See if you can find out what security measures were used. Cade, I want you to conduct exterior surveillance on the house. The usual. Cam locations, alarms, guards, and the daily routines of the staff and Bernard."

"Are you standing down your own additional protection?" Cade asked.

"Yes. Nothing has happened in the two weeks since the accident, so we'll label it a false alarm," Sebastian said. He reached and squeezed Darcelle's hand, giving her a reassuring look.

"Even without that to worry about, Darcelle and I will have to hang back on this job. We don't want Bernard thinking we're watching him. He might not recognize Darcelle, but me? He'd spot me in a heartbeat. Same goes for Max."

Cade pushed his sleeves up. "We'll get the info you need, boss. He won't have a clue we're coming."

Sebastian gestured toward Bassinae. "I've asked Bassinae to come up with a plan for us. Include her on any of the updates you send Darcelle and I."

"Time for the junior varsity to show their stuff." Darcelle grinned like the Cheshire cat at Cade and then winked at Bassinae.

"Junior varsity, my ass."

Darcelle laughed.

Even though Cade's response had been muttered, Sebastian raised an eyebrow at him. Cade huffed and said, "We'll get it done. You don't have to worry about us."

"Just don't go near any dump trucks. Then we will worry."

The pointed look she sent Cade made him lower his gaze to the table. He rubbed his thumb on the wood surface. "Thanks."

"You have your assignments, and I'm ready to spend the evening with my lovely wife. Meeting adjourned." Sebastian rose from his end of the table, took Darcelle by the hand, and left.

"Cheyenne brought back presents for everyone. If you can all come to dinner tomorrow, we'll have a welcome home party at our apartment." Jeanne looked at each of them, getting a nod from Max and Cade.

"We'll be there," Darcelle said.

"I'd love to," Bassinae said. "Do you want me to bring anything?"

"No, we've got it covered." The women continued to talk as they rose from their seats and made their way to the door of the room.

"Uh. Bassinae?"

Everyone, including Max, turned to regard Cade. His brows knit. "I thought if you haven't had supper, we could get a bite... together."

It wasn't like he hadn't asked her to eat with him many times in the past, but somehow this was different. Bassinae had never seen Cade hesitant like this, at least not before the accident. Was he really afraid she would refuse? They had to talk because they couldn't go on this way.

"Sure. How about Gio's down the street?"

"Sounds good." Cade reached to take her elbow and then withdrew his hand, sticking it in his pocket.

Bassinae ignored the wordless communication that shot between Max and Jeanne. Oh yes. She and Cade needed to have a talk.

* * * *

It was still light out, but the sun, on its way to setting, drew long shadows on the sidewalks of the city street. Gio's, a cozy Italian family restaurant, was in the building on the other side of the Banque Populaire.

Cade couldn't believe what a ham-handed ass he had become. Women didn't unnerve him, so why was he acting so skittish around

Bassinae? Getting the girl had always been easy. His good looks did most of the work. Brash charm sealed the deal. But that wouldn't succeed with Bassinae. He couldn't treat her like a one-night stand. She'd kick him so far down the road he'd be in another province.

Wooing, that's what Sebastian had recommended. So I ask her out to supper. But I can't count that as a date. We do that all the time. Make it special. How the hell do you make pizza and a beer special?

His heart skipped a beat when Bassinae took his hand, his whole body soaring with the thrill. He came plummeting to the ground at her words.

"We need to talk."

The ache in the back of his throat made it hard to respond. "Yeah. I—"

Bits of concrete flew at them, and Cade realized the sound he'd heard was a bullet whizzing through the air. Instinctively he snatched Bassinae and pulled her behind one of the huge pillars that fronted the bank. Not that this was completely safe. A shot ricocheted off another pillar, sending more shards of concrete in their direction.

Bassinae had gone ashen, her body crumpled in a ball. Had she been struck badly? A trickle of blood ran down the side of her face. Cade lifted her into his arms and barreled his way over the threshold of the bank, entering before the synthsteel security doors slid shut.

Inside he collapsed to the floor, pulling Bassinae onto his lap. He held her face between his hands and called her name, trying to get past the shock that had left her mute and shaking. "Bassinae. Are you hurt? Tell me where it hurts?" Someone was shouting at him, but he ignored them. He gently dragged his fingers along her arms and sides to her knees. When he did the same to her chest and abdomen, she jerked back with a cry. He lifted her shirt, noting the hole that had been ripped in the fabric, and found where a chunk of concrete had hit her, tearing through her skin and embedding itself in the muscle above her belly button.

"Hands on your head."

The security guard's voice made it through the white noise that filled Cade's ears. "She's been injured. Someone shot at us."

Bassinae was curled in on herself, her fingers pressed tightly to her stomach.

"Both of you, lie facedown on the floor with your hands on your head. Now!"

The man meant business. His weapon never wavered from its aim at Cade's chest. "She's hurt. Please don't shoot her." He moved Bassinae off his lap to lie on her side. "She's got a chunk of concrete in her gut. She can't lie on her stomach. Please don't shoot her."

"Fine. Get on the floor now."

Doing as instructed, Cade said, "I don't have a gun on me, but there's a knife in the sheath in my boot."

Another guard patted Cade down, removing the knife and stepping back. Outside sirens drew closer. A flurry of voices and barked commands announced the arrival of the police. In the few minutes it took for them to secure the scene and take charge from the bank guards, Cade had run over the sequence of events in his mind several times. He replayed the sound of the initial shot. It hadn't been a pistol. But where on this street could anyone use a rifle without being seen? Whoever took the shot must have done so from a window, but the building opposite had none except on the ground level. He would have seen someone shooting from that position. Which meant the gunman had been aiming at an angle and, thank the gods, missed. The two of them had been right out in the open. If the man had waited until they were farther along the street, Bassinae wouldn't have a chunk of rock in her belly. Instead she could be dead.

Her whimpers struck him like blows. How bad was she hurt? He didn't really know. The chunk of concrete was visible, but training told him not to pull it out. But what if it was larger than it looked? Wouldn't there be more blood? Was she bleeding internally? His heart racing, it took all Cade's self-control to resist going to her. "It's okay, Bassinae. Help's coming. I know it hurts, but they'll fix you up and you'll be just fine." *Gods, let that be true.*

A gruff voice sounded close by, and the tips of polished cowboy boots came into Cade's view. "This the pair?"

"Yeah. It looks like someone shot at them. They ran inside before the door closed. Once it did, the shooting stopped."

"I'll need the vids."

"Yes, sir. The woman is injured."

"Med tech. Over here, help her." The man nudged Cade's elbow with the toe of his boot. "You. On your feet. Slow."

Cade stood, keeping his hands on his head.

"You can drop your hands." The detective peered at Cade long and hard. "So why would someone want to shoot you or the young lady?"

Fists clenched at his sides, Cade shook his head. "No idea. Unless it has something to do with Do It Now. Bassinae works there. Maybe some disgruntled husband or boyfriend decided to take potshots at the shelter's staff." It was a theory, but few, other than the women who were helped and the staff at Do It Now, knew Bassinae worked there. Whoever this was, it wasn't likely they were shooting at Bassinae. He was by far a better candidate for a murder attempt. And here he'd started to believe he'd left his past behind.

The detective glanced over at Bassinae where the med tech was checking her over for additional injuries after lightly bandaging her stomach. When he looked back at Cade, he said, "We'll check into that. You sure you have no enemies wanting to take you down? You look like you can handle yourself in a fight."

Now that he knew they wouldn't be shot, Cade had to force down his rising need to shove away from the detective and fall to Bassinae's side, to assure himself that she wasn't badly hurt. He locked his gaze on her, gritting his teeth. "I'm former Special Forces, so yeah, I do have enemies, but I thought they were all dead or off planet. I didn't think anyone hated me enough to come here to kill me." He looked the detective straight in the eye. "Not anyone alive, anyway. I can't tell you any more than that. Can I go to her now?"

"Sure. The officer over there"—he pointed at a woman speaking to the security guards and taking notes on a tablet—"she'll get your information. You'll hear from me."

"Thanks." Cade moved to where Bassinae lay, kneeling at her head. "How is she?"

The med tech said, "She was hit by flying concrete in a few places. Only the one to her abdomen did more than graze the skin."

A bandage covered the spot on Bassinae's forehead where she'd been bleeding. Cade leaned over and gently kissed her next to it. "You're okay, sunshine."

She gazed up at him, her brown eyes brimming with emotion. "You saved me."

His gut clenched. "I'll always save you."

"Sir, let me examine you."

Cade tried to wave the med tech off, but in the end bandages were applied to the gouges in his own skin. He gave the police officer his and Bassinae's names and addresses while he was being treated. After she'd located them in the citizen's database and confirmed what he'd told her, she said he was free to go.

The tech and his coworkers had secured Bassinae to a gurney and were hovering her toward the waiting emergency medical vehicle. Cade rushed to accompany her when he heard a familiar voice directing the EMTs to take Bassinae to the Do It Now clinic. It was Sebastian, taking charge as usual. Cade pushed forward to ride with Bassinae but was stopped by a firm grip on his arm.

"Let him go with her. They'll do what he says."

Cade pulled, attempting to free himself from Max, but the man's resolute expression told Cade it would take more force than he wanted to commit to with police and emergency personnel flooding the area. He nodded his agreement, and Max released him.

"Come on. I brought the rover."

Once they were inside the armored car, Max eased around the vehicles, their lights still flashing, cluttering the street outside the bank. "What the hell happened?"

"No fucking idea." Rather than pound the dashboard, Cade flexed his fingers. "Someone shot at me, or Bassinae, or both of us."

Max pulled into the garage and parked the vehicle in its assigned slot. The ambulance was pulled up to the elevator's glass enclosure, lights flashing. "We'll find out. That's twice now."

"Twice?" It took a moment for the idea to snap into clarity in Cade's mind. "The dump truck."

His voice a deep growl, his expression grim, Max said, "Yeah, the dump truck."

"That was for me?" Cade's thoughts were running at hyperspeed. Who the hell would try to kill him? Three years ago he would have understood, but now?

"Looks like it."

"What the..." Cade ran a hand through his hair.

Max clapped him on the shoulder. "Go see Bassinae. We'll figure this out."

* * * *

Bassinae opened her eyes when she heard Cade's voice, her heart fluttering. Her whole body seemed to radiate light. Somewhere between the bank where the shooting had happened and the clinic, she'd had an epiphany. One that should have occurred when he was the one hurt and the fear of losing him had filled her with darkness. She loved him as more than a best friend. That love had crept up on her, and she, unwilling to look beyond her own blind adherence to her rule against forming romantic relationships, hadn't seen it for what it was. She'd been on her way to Gio's with him to remind him of that absolute truth. Thank the gods she hadn't had the opportunity.

"Hey, Miss Mary."

"Hey." The word drifted past her lips in a long, winding stream of sound. She and the entire room were floating. Every direction she cast her gaze, wondrously delightful things appeared. The sheets on her bed were glistening white. The blinds at the window glimmered with the sunbeams that gently touched each slat. The overhead lampshade was a perfect circle. No sharp edges, no hard surfaces anywhere.

And there was Cade. Such a beautiful man. His dark blonde curls glowed. They would be so much fun to play with. Spiral them around her fingers. Sift them. Smooth them back to stare into his eyes. Beautiful hazel eyes. Beautiful, beautiful man. But his forehead was wrinkled and his body tense. That wasn't right. *I'll smile at him. That will brighten him up.*

She released all the peace and joy she was feeling in the most brilliant smile ever, but he didn't return it. Instead he pressed his lips together and ducked his head. "Come here." She patted the mattress next to her twice, in slow motion. "Sit."

When he'd gingerly positioned himself on the edge of the bed, he still kept his gaze from hers, studying his fingers in his lap. "Bassinae, I—"

"Shhh, beautiful man." She stretched her arm out to touch his face, succeeding in brushing a finger along his jaw, through the wiry hair of his beard. He took hold of her hand, squeezed it, and brought it to his lips, placing a tender kiss on her knuckles.

"I'm sorry. It's my fault you got hurt." His breath heated her fingers.

"Oh, you big dope. You're the one who saved me." A chuckle bubbled inside her, and she set it free to sail and burst over him. "You whisked me to safety. You're my hero."

"No. I'm nothing of the kind. I—"

She gave him an unhurried shake of her finger and grinned. "Don't try to fool me, Cade Johnson. It was you. With those big, strong muscles of yours." She wrapped her arms around herself and gave herself a contented squeeze. "But you're still sad." She dropped her arms. "You shouldn't be sad. Everything is just fine."

"Bassinae—"

"Come here." She reached for him, trying to take his face between her palms. "*Mon beau lion*, come closer. The truth is in my eyes."

When he leaned down and met her gaze, all the happiness she'd been feeling turned to an ache. "Oh, it is not so bad as that." His gaze was dull and lifeless. Something was very wrong, but it was hard to pull her thoughts together. She'd seen that expression before, but when? Early on. When they first met. He'd been full of false bravado, and she'd taken him for an asshole. But then she'd seen this look cross his face, and she'd known. He was full of a stultifying loneliness. And here it was again, marring his rugged beauty. She pulled him closer, pressed her lips softly to his, and whispered, "I love you. I won't let you be alone."

Cade gasped, his neck jerking beneath the fingers she'd clasped around it. Instead of pulling away, he kissed her back. A gentle taking and giving that sent her spirit soaring. A warmth she had forgotten suffused her. The memory of the sensation was buried amid others along with the pain. Now she remembered. The taste of a man's desire. The forging of a new, deeper connection. The throb of need that began in her nipples and bloomed into a full ache between her thighs. When he finally shifted away, a smile spread across her face. He didn't return it. His expression was serious, his gaze intense, revealing what she suspected. Cade Johnson was in love with her. And that was more than all right. She'd moved past the compulsion to exclude intimacy with a man from her life. She wasn't fragile any more. No, she was a strong woman. Hell. She taught other women how to defend themselves.

Cade grimaced and lowered his head and straightened away from her. "I shouldn't have done that. I'm sorry." Keeping his chin on his chest, he looked at her. "You're all loopy on meds, and I took advantage of you, even though I know you don't want me in that way. I'm such a bastard." He dropped his gaze again.

"Oh, beautiful man." Bassinae poured all her love into her words. Because she did love him. Had loved him for a long time, it seemed. "I kissed you. Can't you tell when a woman is trying to seduce you?"

He raised his head. "You're not yourself."

"Ca—"

"No." He pressed one large finger to her lips. "The painkiller you're on has you doing things you'd never do otherwise. You'd never have kissed me." He brushed his knuckles over her cheek. "I guess by now you know I love you. But a relationship between us isn't possible. You don't want it. And my past... I thought I'd left it behind, but it's caught back up to me. Put you in danger. And I can't have that. I can't bear that you were hurt." Damp glistened in his eyes. "If it had been worse, if you had been killed, it would have been the end of me. I'll stay away from you."

All the lightness seeped from Bassinae's body. From floating in blissful happiness, her limbs were now too heavy to lift. The small chunk of concrete had been removed and the hole sealed, but her midsection felt as though another entire block had taken up residence.

He pushed off the bed to stand, but she grabbed his arm to stop him. "Don't do that. I'm sorry I took so long to figure it out. I may be loopy on meds, but I know my heart. It couldn't make itself heard because my mind was so busy repeating the mantra I'd latched on to when I escaped the bastard who beat me. Get it through your thick skull. I love you, Cade. And that's not going to stop when I come back down off this painkiller high."

Cade grimaced. "A week ago I'd have crawled over broken glass to hear you say that. But it doesn't change the underlying truth. We can't be together. I'm too dangerous to be with. I won't be responsible for you getting hurt again." He pulled away from her, and this time she let him go. At the door he turned to look over his shoulder. "Goodbye."

The hell. She didn't tell someone she loved them to have them walk out of her life the next minute. Not happening. The pulsing throb of pain from her wound was slipping into her awareness. She flicked the button that gave her another hit of happy juice. First she would get well, and then she'd go drag Cade kicking and screaming back into her life.

Chemical bliss seeped through her veins, creating a faux rosiness to the situation. She chuckled in the back of her throat. A better idea had come to her. She would seduce that hunk of sexy man. *I'm his massage therapist. I know just which buttons to push.*

Once again she was floating. She drifted off to sleep with a smile on her lips.

CHAPTER FIVE

CADE SELDOM ENTERED Jeanne's domain on the eighth floor of the high-rise. It reminded him too much of the world of high-tech gear, armor, and weapons he'd left behind when he was unceremoniously dismissed from the fleet. After the debacle on Undoa Prime, he hadn't been able to climb back into a suit of battle armor. The panic attacks that resulted from every attempt and the stain on his record had finished his career. Although he'd been given an honorable discharge for medical reasons and he'd been cleared of all wrongdoing, his name was so solidly linked to the atrocity that it had been impossible to find security work. Until Sebastian had contacted him.

The comm call from Sebastian asking Cade to become his personal security guard had been a miracle, saving Cade from a life as a short-order cook in a greasy hole-in-the-wall that should have been closed for health violations. It paid to be a homeboy on the same planet as Sebastian St. Croix. At least for Cade it had.

Turning from a piece of surveillance equipment she was tinkering with, Jeanne said, "Hey, big boy. Looks like someone really hates you."

Cade grunted, pulled out a chair from the work table, and sat opposite Jeanne. "Yeah. And I need to know who."

"I went over Max's work on the truck accident when I got home. There was nothing to tie any of it to Sebastian. We should have been comparing it to your life." She slid a tablet over to Cade. "Go through the file I've brought up and tell me if any of the names ring a bell for you. Go through the images too."

Cade dragged the tablet to him with one finger, picked it up, and settled back to read. The file was a complete dossier on the trucking company and its employees and the same for the parking garage. None of the people in charge of either could explain why the truck had been in the garage in the first place. It had been scheduled to be three blocks over at a construction site, hauling debris from a building that was being torn down. The CEO of the trucking firm had insisted that there'd been some kind of glitch in the auto-drive programming of the vehicle, assumed full responsibility, and considered the matter closed.

Sebastian didn't let it lie there. He'd gotten a subpoena for the truck's black box, which showed that the vehicle's prescribed path had been set to send it to the construction site, but partway there had diverted to the garage to wait until the moment he and Cade had driven along the road.

The next page in the file was a list of the trucking company's employees with ID photos. Running his finger down the column, Cade scrutinized each individual. His eyes widened. That man. Cade enlarged the image. With the beard it was hard to say. The name didn't ring a bell.

"Did you find something?"

Cade looked up at Jeanne. "Maybe. This guy seems familiar."

"What's his name?"

"Adam Smith."

Jeanne rolled her chair over to her keyboard and tapped.

"I don't know anyone by that name though." Cade rubbed his jaw. "But if he weren't wearing this beard... I don't know... He looks like a guy from my unit on Undoa Prime. But I thought that guy was dead."

"Well, there's a bunch of Adam Smith's to choose from. How old would he be?"

"Mid thirties."

"And the name of your buddy in the fleet?"

"Not my buddy. Definitely not my buddy. Paul Nordgren. I thought he was a casualty in the Undoa Prime atrocity."

Jeanne brought an image up on the wall vidscreen and gestured. "That him?"

"Yeah. That's Nordgren. He was one of the dipshits that ran amuck and slaughtered all those civilians. That was such a clusterfuck. Most of those soldiers wouldn't have dreamed of doing something like that. Half of them were new to the field. Babies, really. They got caught up in the moment, the panic, and just reacted. But that guy..." Cade stabbed a finger toward the vidscreen. "That guy would have happily set the whole thing off, not caring who died. Civilians, the enemy, our own side. He, along with a couple of other guys in the unit, were bad seeds. One of them disabled my battle armor and left me lying there helpless to stop what happened. I'm probably lucky they didn't frag me." Anger rushed through him like an electric current, the same visceral reaction he always got when he remembered that day.

"Damn." Jeanne's voice gentled. "I didn't know. I mean, I knew that you'd been there and were the officer in charge, but I didn't know any details. Just that you'd been absolved of all wrongdoing and Sebastian vouched for you."

Cade turned his head to focus on a stack of equipment in the corner. "I appreciate what Sebastian did more than you can believe. Most people never remember that I was found not guilty, or they think I got away with pinning it on the men below me." Cade grimaced and slid a glance at Jeanne before looking away again. "I'll never forget that day. We were clearing a section of the city that the enemy had pulled out of. Sometimes they would leave wounded soldiers behind to try to take us out. There was a kid, maybe twelve, sitting against the wall of his apartment building. Didn't look good. With a kid that age, you assume the worst because it was often true. Probably a fighter. Probably wounded. He had a rifle on his lap.

"I was on the far side of the street leading a team through those buildings. Goshwond Moparu, my lieutenant, was in charge of the team that found the boy. He told the kid in Standard to set the rifle aside, but when the boy picked it up, it swung toward them. Someone fired. Killed the kid. Goshwond ordered cease-fire, but the kid's mother ran from the building with her own weapon, a huge rifle, and attacked him. Hit him in the faceplate, shattered it. He went down with shrapnel to his right cheek. Lost an eye. Someone shot and killed her.

"Then all hell broke loose. Civilians poured out of the buildings, attacking us with whatever weapons they had on hand, and someone shot out my power unit. I fell flat on my face unable to move, unable to make my orders heard. Somebody grabbed the leg of my suit and dragged me into cover, and I thought things would settle down. And then the bombing started. Someone called in an airstrike. Said we'd been ambushed. I couldn't communicate with anyone. I was trapped in that suit for hours. But I knew what a barrage of air-to-surface missiles felt like when they detonated close to your position. Four hundred fifty-two civilians were killed in that massacre. And I could do nothing to stop it." Cade ran a hand through his hair. His voice rough, he poked a finger toward the vidscreen and said, "That guy was on Goshwond's team. If anyone took that first shot, it was that man right there."

"Holy crap. I didn't think you could take out the power unit on battle armor."

He turned to face her. "Not easy. You can only do it by sticking a weapon up and into the shell."

Her eyebrows knit, Jeanne scowled. "Up close and personal then."

"Yeah." Cade realized he was gritting his teeth and relaxed his jaw. "They never proved who did it or who fired the first shot. But there was plenty of blame to go around for everyone once the shooting began. Goshwond, myself, and two others who attempted to stop things were the only ones to come out of the debacle without prison sentences. They still court-martialed us. It looked like the fix was in, but in the end they found the four of us not guilty. Paul Nordgren never came to trial, so I assumed he'd been killed. They kept us locked in solitary, so I didn't get a lot of information back then."

"It says here, he didn't die in the massacre itself. He was shot by a sniper returning to your base camp."

"Huh. Well then Adam Smith can't be Paul Nordgren."

"No, but what about a relative? Let me do a search." She entered the parameters and then leaned back to wait, watching him intently.

"So, what's up with you and Bassinae?"

"Nothing. There is nothing up." Cade leveled a fierce look at Jeanne.

"That's not what I hear. Rumor has it that you are smitten with her, and she's just as stuck on you."

"Well, rumor is wrong. We're friends and nothing more. Nothing. More."

Jeanne held her hands up. "Protest all you want, but she's perfect for you. The only woman on the planet who'd put up with your attitude."

"I do not have an attitude."

"Whatever, big fella. She'd be good for you, and as crazy as it sounds, I think you'd be good for her. So don't blow it."

Before Cade could respond, Jeanne said, "Here we go." She sat forward. "Well, looky here." Another picture appeared next to the image of Paul Nordgren.

"That's him. That's Adam Smith."

"Except he's not Adam Smith. He's Jason Nordgren, Paul's brother." Jeanne swiveled her chair and, eyebrows drawn together, looked directly at Cade. "Just released from Clairvaux Prison. B and E, assault with a deadly. But more to the point, he was part of an auto theft ring that hacked the auto-drive security Citroën installed in their high-end vehicles. They'd take over from the driver or auto-drive of a car, pull it over, and then jack it, leaving the passengers on the side of the road."

"Fuck. I'll bet dump trucks are even easier to hijack." His throat constricted. *I'd like to show this guy the front end of a dump truck.*

Jeanne tilted her head. "Maybe. Maybe not. Still doesn't explain how he knew where you'd be."

"I didn't plan to be on that street. Got off the thruway because of traffic and switched another street over because of a jam-up in an intersection ahead of me." He glanced at her with one eyebrow cocked. "You don't think...?"

Jeanne nodded. "Yeah, I do think. It doesn't take much to stack up the thruway or back up an intersection. This guy obviously has buddies he can call in for help. So that part would be easy peasy. But we still don't know how he figured out you'd be coming that way."

Cade tipped his head to the side and weighed the possibilities. "How could he? Sebastian commed me the night before that his mom was returning early and he wanted to pick her up at the spaceport. He told me to have the sedan ready at nine thirty in the morning. Darcelle and Max probably knew, but it's not like we advertise what we're doing."

Jeanne bit her lip, tapping out a rhythm with her fingertips on the tabletop before ending with a final firm thump. "When's the last time your comm nanites were upgraded?"

"Six months ago."

"Damn." Jeanne slumped. "Not recent enough. He was still in prison. Could have had someone else do the job, but too early and you might get notified of a real upgrade." She looked his way. "Let me guess. You were called about something going wrong with the batch for your last upgrade and you needed to come in for a booster?"

Cade's chest tightened. "Yeah. I got a comm from the clinic. Had to go to an office on the east side. One of those rent-by-the-day places. A doc and med tech. But the doc's lab coat had his and the nano-med company's names on it."

"How long ago?"

"Three days before the accident," Cade said, his whole body taut.

"That's how they did it. Tapped into your comms."

Cade abruptly pushed away from the table and stood, pacing one direction and then the other in the limited space Jeanne's cluttered workspace allowed. "I can't believe I fell for that. They tell you to watch out for scams that offer upgrades to your nanites, but I never..." He turned, his face fierce. "You gotta get these outta me. Now!"

Palms out before her, Jeanne said, "Slow down, stud. Look, anyone could be taken in by this. You thought your doctor called. Told you to go to this office the nanite company had set up to administer a fix."

The glare Cade directed at her would peel paint, Cade responded. "Yeah. I'll bet you wouldn't."

"I am smarter than you, big boy."

The smirk she sent him did nothing to pacify Cade's need to strangle something. "I'll assume then that it will be, what's your term, easy peasy to get these things out of me."

Jeanne narrowed her eyes. "On that. We should let them hang around a bit longer. They used them to set you up. Let's do the same to them. Sebastian will want in on this, but I think we could cook up something to get this guy off your back permanently."

Cade crossed his arms over his chest. "Huh. What do you have in mind?"

"Well, first I'll need to check your nanites to be certain that's what's happened. And then..."

Cade sat and leaned his head toward Jeanne's. Sending the man to prison again couldn't happen soon enough. And once that was done... Maybe his life wasn't as wrecked as he'd thought. This wasn't some crazy-assed vigilante eliminating everyone involved in the atrocity. Take this fucker out and he could get on with priority number one, Bassinae.

* * * *

It had been three days since Bassinae had seen Cade. He'd been pulled from work and commanded to lie low, but that didn't include avoiding her. With their apartments side by side, there hadn't been a three-day period that she didn't at least catch a glimpse of him. Enough was enough. She rapped sharply on his door and waited.

When she got no response, she pounded. "Cade Johnson, you open this door. I know you're in there. Max told me you were home." She thumped some more. "Damn it, Cade. Let me in."

The door swung open. Cade stood in the gap, wearing nothing but low-slung jeans, his hand high on the jamb. "What?"

She scowled up at him. "We need to talk."

"Not now." His voice was rough, as though he'd been sleeping.

"Yes, now. If you won't let me in, I'll stand out here and shout what I have to say."

He grunted, dropped his arm, and swung away from the door. "Fine." He paced into his living room and fell onto the oversize tan couch that filled one wall. His legs stretched out before him, he propped a foot on a padded coffee table and draped his fingers over the end of the armrest.

She stood before him, hands braced on her hips. "Not even going to ask how I am?"

"I know how you are. Max gives me a report every day."

When she continued to glare at him without saying a word, he asked, "How are you?"

"I'm fine. I don't even have a scar." She moved around the coffee table to perch on it next to his foot. He watched her, his gaze roving her body, desire obvious in his heated expression. "Why are you avoiding me?"

He yanked his gaze from her and focused on his fingers, rubbing and pinching the fabric of the armrest. "I will not put you in danger again. Until this thing gets solved, I'm not going near you."

She snorted. "How dangerous would it be to walk thirty steps and visit me. You don't even have to leave the building."

In a rush he dropped his feet to the floor and sat up straight, leaning in toward her. "Gods, Bassinae. Don't you think I want to be with you? Don't you think I worry about you? But I can't. Not yet. Not while this guy is taking potshots at me. And not until I put him on the shelf for good."

"And how long will that be? I want to be with you now. Damn it, Cade. I've made this earthshaking turnabout. I'm ready for a relationship, a romantic relationship, with a man. And that man is you. I know you want it too, so give me my touching and kissing. I want to love you, and I don't want to wait. I'm a big girl, I can handle the bad things in your life, but I can't take you shutting yourself off from me. Not now. Not when everything in me screams to hold you close."

Cade rose to his feet, reached out, and lifted her from the coffee table. His arms swept around her to pull her tight against his chest, and his eyes latched on to hers, full of fervent hunger and burning urgency. She met his gaze with equal intensity, wrapping her legs about his waist and sliding her fingers into the hair on the sides of his head to cradle it between her palms. Without a doubt she had roused her lion from his slumber.

"All right."

The words rasped out past his sensual lips, sending a rush of electricity through her. Then his mouth was on hers, tasting, teasing, making her want more. She tilted her head and opened to his invitation, fascinated by the tang of him as his tongue licked and probed. The icy fingers of fear were gone. This man loved her, protected her, and needed her. *Why the hell did I wait so long for this?* The urge to tear into something, to release the anger that simmered inside, was nearly overwhelming. So she crushed herself to him, grasping his hair and tugging.

One of his hands caressed her rump, stroking and squeezing while the other clutched her in a grip she couldn't break even if she'd wanted to. Which she didn't. She'd never felt such fierce aggression, always believed herself to be gentle through and through, but in this moment she'd very much prefer to shred his clothes from his body, slam him to the floor, and have her way with him. The revelation of the passion coursing through her sparked an inner jubilation. *I'm free. Free of all the crap I've let other men load me down with. Free to love this man the way he deserves to be loved. Uninhibited. Unhindered by the past.*

She pulled her lips from his and smiled with savage delight. "I think you just obliterated Miss Mary Sunshine."

His eyes crinkled, and he chuckled. "Nah, she's a lioness at heart." He moved around the coffee table and strode to his bedroom, where he placed her crosswise on his bed. His brow wrinkled, and he pointed at her stomach. "I don't want to hurt you. Maybe this isn't a good idea."

"You've always been a pain in the ass; I don't expect that to change."

"That's not what I mean."

"I know. And yes, I'm good to go." She thumped her stomach with her palm. "See. You of all people should know nanite repair works fast."

He grunted, but he didn't move from where he stood, towering above her. His gaze roamed over her, lingering, building a tension inside her.

The cool of the coverlet quickly warmed. Impatience tightened its grasp on her need to be touched again. "What are you waiting for?"

"You've never looked at me like this before. I want to remember it."

She'd never seen him like this either, eyes dilated, face taut with desire, the image of restrained sensuality. But it wasn't enough. "Time's up. Make some more memories."

He grinned with a lecherous gleam and lowered himself over her. He traced her eyebrows, the ridge of her cheekbone, and down her nose with his finger, coming to a stop over her lips. He pressed, and she opened, sucking the tip. "Gods, you're beautiful. You make me hard. Feel that." He shifted to brush his erection against her thigh.

After one last swipe of her tongue, she bit him. "A girl couldn't miss that huge piece of man flesh." A puff of a laugh escaped her, followed by a taunting grin.

"Are you trying to tease me?" He smirked at her. "I warn you, I fight dirty."

"Prove it, big boy." All merriment fled, leaving her immersed in churning arousal. His lips devoured her, and his hands roved over her, stroking her neck, smoothing up her side to cup her breast, and slipping beneath her bottom to pull her against his cock so he could grind against her.

She was panting for air when he lifted off her to tug her sports tank over her head. The wet warmth of his mouth trailed down her neck, along her collarbone, and finally where she wanted it most, to her breast. The man was a marvel, skillfully sucking, tonguing, and

67

nipping until she was writhing beneath him, arching up hard, fingers enmeshed in his golden-brown curls, tightening and releasing as sharp bursts of pleasure zipped to her clit.

Raw and primal emotion scudded through her. This man was taking her to a place she'd never known existed. One where hearts, minds, and bodies could meld, become one, each meeting the other's needs in a dance that had persisted since there had been a man and a woman capable of lowering the walls around their hearts. She'd never given so much or received so much. Cade held her heart. The damage he could do to her far exceeded anything that Jessil had meted out with his fists. In the past such thoughts would have made her retch. But she had a guarantee. Cade had also handed her his heart to keep, a rare and wondrous gift she'd never imagined anyone would ever offer her. *Gods, I love this man.*

"I need you inside me now." She barely recognized the growl that was her voice.

Cade grunted, beyond words. He stood over her, his lips parted, and peeled her exercise pants down her hips, pausing to slide her shoes off before freeing her legs. A moment later he was nude, his cock jutting out, fully aroused, the tip damp with precum. He slid over her, pushing her knees up and positioning his erection at the juncture of her thighs, pulsing forward until he found her entrance. Then he thrust home in one long, nerve-expanding stroke.

"Feel. So. Good. Fuck, Bassinae, I love you." When he moved, Bassinae could do nothing but cling to him, moaning and arching to meet each thrust. She strove, struggling to reach a peak that seemed to wait just out of her grasp, a summit that was always a little higher. She trusted him to get her there, submerging herself in the slide of his straining muscles between her thighs, his warm skin beneath her hands, and his cock filling her, completing her. He kissed her, consuming her mouth while he pierced her deeply and thoroughly, using his powerful muscles to bind them together. She hit the pinnacle and flew, crying out, her whole body suffused with light and bliss. Wrapped around him, pleasure leaked from every pore when he roared his own release, pulsing inside her, his fingers gripping her hips.

For several minutes she lay melted beneath him, luxuriating in his weight atop her, wishing to remain forever connected to him. He pushed up on one elbow and stroked her face, tugging on a dread. "That was amazing. I love you, Bassinae." He gently kissed her and then rolled them to their sides, continuing to run a lazy finger over her skin.

She smiled at him.

His grin was gentle. "Ah, there's Miss Mary Sunshine."

The swat she aimed at his arm never made contact. He slipped a hand behind her head and brought her to him, kissing her deeply enough to prove that his passion hadn't diminished. He pushed her onto her back, and said, "I haven't gotten to taste all of you yet. You rushed me."

"Big boy, nobody's gonna rush you, if you don't want to be rushed."

He smirked at her. "True. And I think I'm going to be taking my time with this." He covered her nipple with his mouth, sucking and then giving it a nip.

"Oh." Who was she to stop him? They could worry about their problems later.

CHAPTER SIX

CADE PILED HIS plate with sausage, eggs, bacon, and hash browns and then took another, heaping a stack of pancakes on it. Once he'd thoroughly drenched them in syrup, he carried both plates to the breakfast table where the rest of the team was already eating. He slid into the chair next to Bassinae, smiling at her and reaching under the table to squeeze her knee. The sexy smirk she flashed at him made his groin tighten. Images of her naked and wanton beneath him ran through his mind. When her eyes grew heated, it was apparent she was having similar thoughts. He arched an eyebrow at her.

"Jeez, Cade. Even with my metabolism and a healthy dose of fat-fighting nanites, I can't eat like that." Jeanne waved her fork at the mounds of food Cade had in front of him.

His gaze swiveled to Jeanne, and he shoveled an enormous bite into his mouth. After swallowing, he said, "I've told you before. My body is a finely tuned machine. I don't use nanites to stay in shape. Never needed them. Besides, you know Darcelle doesn't allow anything that's not optimized nutritionally on her table."

"It's the quantity, not the quality, lunkhead."

"If you'll notice"—he waved a hand at himself and then at her—"there's more of me than there is of you."

"You think—"

"Enough. Can't a man eat breakfast in peace?" Max glared at them. Everyone stopped and looked up at his outburst.

"Everything all right, Max?" Sebastian asked. "You seem on edge of late."

"I'm fine. Ready to get down to business." He dropped his gaze to his plate, scraping the remaining gravy into a mound.

Sebastian shared a look with Darcelle before continuing. "Okay then. I called you all here because as you know, we have a problem. Jeanne, explain what you and Cade discovered."

Cade started on his pancakes, leaning forward with each bite to avoid dripping syrup on his shirt. Jeanne described who was behind the attacks and how Cade's inner comm had been hacked. He looked at each person sitting around the table while she did. They had become his family, replacing the military, which had been his family since the age of sixteen when his parents died. A two-year stint in a prep academy had been followed by boot camp and then special-ops training. He'd expected eventually to leave the fleet behind. He'd never imagined the fleet would boot him before he was ready.

This family was different. A big brother, sisters. A wise old uncle. Although Max would probably pop him for the *old*. And then there was Bassinae, in a category all by herself. These people wouldn't abandon him, even though he'd put them all in danger. When Cade had broached the need to leave to protect the others, Sebastian had stopped him cold. His heart couldn't feel any fuller than it did right now.

The turn of his thoughts must have shown on Cade's face. Sebastian gave him a light tap on his shoulder and said, "We're going to remove this threat from your life. That's a promise."

Cade cleared his throat before responding, brushing a hand under his nose. "Thank you." He trailed his gaze around the table. "Everyone."

They each offered him a nod or a look of determination and sympathy. Bassinae's was tinged with worry.

"It's been four days since the last attempt. We don't know what he'll try next, but it's certain if Cade makes one step out of this building, that this guy will be on him." Sebastian pointed at Jeanne. "What have you found out about him?"

"I sent a package to each of you. It includes a bunch of images of Jason Nordgren. Study them, please. After his recent release from prison, he's been in the wind. Served the full ten-year sentence, so no parole. He's a member of the Unione Corse, married into one of the

71

families. Mid-level. His specialty is motor vehicle theft. Started out carjacking. Got pulled into running a chop shop. Did time for that. Has other minors for assault and battery, bar fights mostly but also known to slap his girlfriends around. Never made that mistake with his wife. But then they'd kill him if he did. He has two kids. Little girls. Adorable actually. If the family was behind taking you out, Cade, you'd already be dead. So he's working alone or with a buddy or two."

Sebastian took over. "From the pattern of his actions so far, he planned his first attempt in detail while he was still in prison. But once it failed, he had to switch out of his comfort zone. Probably spent time firing a sniper rifle on the range, but he doesn't seem like the type of individual with the ability for mental or physical calm. So his shots went wide. He's frustrated and more likely to make stupid decisions. Let's hear ideas. Anyone?" Sebastian said.

Darcelle held her fork paused before her lips, a slice of peach speared to the tines. "How are we going to fix this? We can't just murder the guy."

"The comm hack can be used to set him up, though," Jeanne said. "He wants to kill Cade. Let's give him an opportunity he can't resist. Then we can move in, take him down, and call the police in."

Bassinae glared and raised her voice. "What? Put Cade out like a sitting duck and let him get shot for real? No way. Not happening."

For a second everyone at the table stared at Bassinae. Jeanne blinked and then narrowed her eyes, considering Bassinae, her lips quirking into a knowing smirk.

Cade turned his gaze on Bassinae. Her eyebrows were pulled together, creating a crease on her forehead. Alarm shone from her eyes, and her jaw was set in rigid denial. He reached under the table again and smoothed his hand over her knee. "It's actually a good idea. Get him where we control the scene."

She tilted her head, but before the word *no* could drop from her lips, Sebastian said, "We can be there to make sure no harm comes to Cade. But we need evidence of attempted murder. Even this guy can't be stupid enough to try something in front of police eyes, which means we'll have to bring the police to him."

"I can help with that," Max said.

"Will your friend on the force go along with us?" Sebastian asked. "I'd prefer to handle the setup ourselves. I don't want this taken out of our hands, so the police can muck it up."

Max eyed Sebastian, a scowl on his face, and pushed his plate away. "If that's what you want. I can tell him I have something to show him. He'll come. I've done it before. Always lead to big busts. Getting him to the location won't be a problem."

"We make this happen and this guy will be out of Cade's life for good. One more major felony and he'll be sent to the ultra max on the moon. You don't come back from there," Jeanne said.

"I'll work out the details of the setup. Jeanne, I'll probably need you for some tech work. Other than that, ladies, you're out of this."

Darcelle's expression went rigid. "That's not the way we work."

"For this, it is." Sebastian met Darcelle's stare and held it, neither willing to be the one to break.

"He's right, Darcelle." Max's composed voice cut through the tension. "This will be far more dangerous. Let the men handle this. We can't afford to have our focus split worrying about you."

"You don't—"

Max raised a hand. "We would, and you know it."

In the seconds that followed, it appeared that Darcelle would refuse to budge on the issue. Then she crossed her arms over her chest with a huff and said, "All right. I'll keep my nose out of this."

Sebastian knew better than to reach a conciliatory hand out to Darcelle. "Thank you. The sooner we take Nordgren down, the sooner we can get to work on the Bernard jewelry heist." Sebastian stood from his end of the table. "Once I have my plan in place, we'll set things in motion."

Cade grabbed another biscuit, tossing it in the air and catching it. Things might turn out all right.

* * * *

73

During the drive out to the warehouse, Cade had plenty of time to go over every part of the plan. As usual, Sebastian had covered all the angles. Still sitting here in the semidarkness just outside the bright glow from a light pole thirty feet away, Cade sensed the ghost pressure of an imaginary bullet between his shoulder blades. They'd set this up as another sniper attempt since Nordgren had already proven an awful shot. But he could always get lucky. Sebastian, Max, and his friendly policeman, Simon, had taken their positions twelve hours prior to Cade's arrival. They'd set up a two-way, since his comm was compromised. If they said Nordgren wasn't here, he wasn't.

The worry now was, why wasn't he here? He should have established himself hours ago. You didn't arrive to a sniper attack late. So here Cade sat, early evening, in a car parked between two warehouses, solid walls on either side of him with no windows opening on the alley. A description of this exact spot between the warehouses had been included in the exchange of comms with Sebastian the night before. The opportunity had been handed to Nordgren tied up in a bow.

Maybe he'd decided it was too easy, and thus a trap. It was, after all, a convoluted setup. Sebastian was supposedly driving to the site with a buyer he was taking on a walk-through of the warehouse. Cade was supposed to park out of sight of the main entrance to chauffeur Sebastian home afterward. Although why Cade was told to hide his presence was never addressed. Sebastian had said it wouldn't matter, but maybe it had. Or maybe they hadn't given Nordgren enough time to take advantage of the situation? Whatever the reason, the *maybes* were damn unsettling now that they didn't know where the man was or what he was planning.

A trickle of sweat ran down Cade's side beneath the cotton shirt he wore. Through his windshield he could see the building across the way, the facade lit crisp as day by another streetlight. The second-floor window was one of the three perfect sniper locations available for Nordgren to choose from. But the shade covering it hadn't so much as twitched. Max claimed no one had entered that building.

Which left the roof above and the stack of cargo containers at the far end of this alley. Sebastian had had the large metal boxes moved to block the alley partially at the back ends of the warehouses.

A shot from above would be hard. The car's roof was no barrier, but it would be difficult to determine where Cade was in the vehicle. A miss and the target could drive away. Breaking into the building across the way was problematic for other reasons, so they figured that Nordgren would pick the position carefully prepared for him. Two rows of containers stacked two high had been positioned so a narrow path ran between the rows. A gap, wide enough to aim a rifle through, was left where the containers in the row closest to the alley butted end to end. It gave the impression of cover, but Sebastian had Jeanne install several tiny surveillance cameras. Once Cade arrived and Nordgren raised his rifle, Jeanne had rigged a flash bang to take him out. Then Sebastian, Max, and the police officer would burst from their hiding place and arrest Nordgren.

But Nordgren hadn't shown.

Cade drummed the fingers of his left hand on the steering wheel and tightened his grip on his Glock 169. He'd chosen it for its ability to drop a man in a wide variety of circumstances. It was one of his first major purchases after leaving his military-grade weapons behind when he and the fleet parted ways. If he had to go civilian, a Glock 169 was an excellent substitute.

The two-way pinged. "A truck's coming, bobtailing. No trailer attached. Probably here to pick up a container already loaded on a flatbed from another warehouse." Max didn't sound concerned.

"Roger. It is an industrial park," Cade responded.

"It's heading your direction, but it's not slowing. Looks like he's headed past you to someplace on the far side. Keep your eyes open."

"Will do."

Cade flexed the fingers of his gun hand, his gaze trained on the spot where he would first catch sight of the truck. He didn't have long to wait, but rather than zip past, the vehicle came to a screeching stop. Under the full illumination of the streetlight, Jason Nordgren's face was immediately identifiable. For a split second the two men stared at

HOW TO STEAL THE PHARAOAH'S JEWELS

one another, and then Nordgren turned away, reaching for something on the seat beside him. Reacting from sheer instinct, Cade barreled out of the car. His military training fully kicked in, he took aim at Nordgren even as the man raised a shoulder-launched missile. Cade shot six times in rapid succession on autopilot. The first bullet struck Nordgren in the chest. Two more hit off center to the right, while the fourth obliterated his face. The remaining bullets were later accounted for as ricochets off the missile itself.

What. The. Fuck? Cade's pulse was pounding even as he struggled to breathe evenly. *A missile. Tried to kill me with a missile.* He must have missed the sound of the container door being flung open, because as he stood panting with a hand on his chest and the other dangling at his side still holding the gun, the trio rushed up and startled him. The police officer, whatever his name was, went straight to the truck.

Sebastian's laugh was loud and raucous. He pounded Cade on the back. "That was some shooting. I would've sworn it was over for all of us. The cameras from the front of the warehouse showed he was stopping. When we saw Nordgren pull that missile onto his shoulder, we hauled ass out of that container. By the time we came around into the alley, you'd already taken him down. Gods, I can't wait to watch it on vid." He hurried toward the truck, leaving Cade in Max's care.

All the energy drained from Cade in a sudden flush. He bent over at the waist, both hands on his knees, including the one still grasping the pistol.

"You gonna hurl?" Max asked, rubbing Cade's back but staying well away from the danger zone if

Cade's stomach decided it had had enough.

"No." Cade huffed the response out.

"Let me take that." Max pried the weapon from his hand. "Simon will want to impound it. I'll hold on to it for him."

Cade stood back up. "Yeah. Thanks."

"Let's sit in the car."

Cade nodded and let Max usher him into the driver's seat. After Max had gone around the car and climbed into the passenger side, the two sat silently, Cade still breathing harshly, waiting for the numbness to clear. He wasn't a stranger to his body's reaction after a violent, near-death encounter. But neither had he stared certain death straight in the face before.

He closed his eyes, and an image of Bassinae appeared in his mind, glaring as she had when using Cade as bait had first been suggested. *She's gonna be pissed.* He shuffled the glowering picture away, replacing it with one of her with a brilliant smile. That was the woman he'd fallen in love with, Miss Mary Sunshine. And then the seductress he'd discovered when they first made love materialized, with a teasing smirk on her lips. *Gods.* He dragged a hand over his face. More than anything he wanted to get home and fuck her until he couldn't move. She was his now. For keeps. She'd overcome her fear of getting involved with another man who could hurt her, and he'd prevailed over his past. The future was theirs to create.

In contemplating Bassinae, all the mental aftershocks from the shooting had melted away. The heaviness was gone. If he weren't sitting in a car, he could probably jump ten feet in the air. He grinned and glanced at Max. Then did a double take. Max was leaning, elbow on the armrest, chin resting on his index finger curled slightly higher than the rest of his fist, a pose meant to express relaxed thoughtfulness. Except that his other hand was fisted tight on his thigh, and anyone more than casually acquainted with Max would detect the tension in a body that normally flowed with the grace of a dancer.

"You're mad."

Max didn't look at Cade when he responded. "Not at you."

The implication that he shouldn't pursue it was clear. Cade let silence fall around them again. If Max was angry, it was at himself or Sebastian. Either way, he'd let the two of them hammer it out.

More police and an ambulance arrived in a flurry of lights and sirens. Soon the whole area was cordoned off. They were asked to exit the car and sent to wait by a police vehicle. A few minutes later Sebastian joined them. After twenty minutes each of them was pulled aside to give a statement. Cade's fingerprints and DNA were taken, and his hands were tested for residue from firing a gun. Finally, with admonitions to make themselves available for further inquiries, they were released.

"This way." Sebastian waved them toward the car he'd called to pick them up. The driver opened the passenger door for Sebastian. "Thanks for not letting Darcelle know you were coming, George."

"No problem, Mr. St. Croix."

Max took the front passenger seat, so Cade piled into the rear to sit with Sebastian.

"You might as well tell me what's got your nose out of joint," Sebastian said, staring at the back of Max's head.

George's shoulders stiffened, and he made a concerted effort to stare straight ahead. Cade couldn't blame him. He didn't really want to be around for a falling out between Sebastian and Max, but neither was he about to turn his head aside to offer them a veil of privacy.

"Well?"

Max turned, arm on the top of his seat, hand resting on George's seat back, and glared at Sebastian. "You nearly got us all killed. Not just one of us, but every single gods damned man of us. Did you stop to think about Darcelle, or Jeanne and Cheyenne? What about your mother, your father, and your brother? When are you going to learn that you aren't invincible, nor are you incapable of screwing the pooch?"

His body thrust back into the seat as though he'd been struck, Sebastian didn't reply. He stared at Max, his forehead wrinkled and his jaw working. Sebastian sat for long moments in the heavy silence that had fallen, his lips pressed into a narrow line. Finally he spoke. "You're right. I apologize. I let hubris overcome my common sense and put us all in danger."

Despite the apology, Max wasn't done venting. "You should have let the police handle this. Simon wanted to put a tail on Nordgren. You wouldn't let him. We'd have known the guy was coming in the truck. But no, you have to make everything so fucking complicated. Guy can't shoot for crap. He didn't even bother to come out and check the site. Just got a bigger gun. One that couldn't miss. We'd have known that if someone was tailing him."

"You're absolutely correct. I got in over my head. I should stick to what I do best." A tinge of heat came into Sebastian's eyes. "If you thought I was heading us over a cliff, why didn't you say something before we got here tonight?"

Max glared at Sebastian. "You're right. I should have. I was distracted. Along for the ride and no more, and that's my fault." Max pointed his finger at Sebastian. "We'll both do better in future."

Reaching forward to grasp Max's hand, Sebastian said, "That we will. I promise to simplify if you promise to warn me about my less brilliant ideas."

Max grunted his agreement.

"All right then," Sebastian said, settling back.

The answering response came from the front seat. "All right."

Both men turned their heads to stare out a window, and Cade sighed. Max's anger would be nothing compared to the explosion that Darcelle would set off when they got back to the penthouse. What was the chance he could grab Bassinae and escape before Darcelle hit the trigger?

Yeah, not good.

CHAPTER SEVEN

THE WOMEN AWAITED them in the penthouse. Sebastian had commed to say they were arriving when the car entered the high-rise's garage. Upon walking into the living room, three distinct impressions struck Cade. Darcelle was standing, fists on hips poised for a free-for-all. Jeanne was stretched out, legs crossed at the ankles, lacking only a bag of popcorn to be ready for the show. And Bassinae—well, she was running full tilt at him.

She plastered herself to him, burying her face in his chest with such force he had to step back to keep them upright. Beneath his arms, wrapped tightly around her, she was sobbing. He stroked her head, murmuring, "It's okay. Everything's okay."

Steel in her voice, Darcelle said to Max, "Thank you. I'll take things from here."

He cast a glance, his eyes dark, at Sebastian and then returned his gaze to Darcelle, giving her a half bow. Without a word he turned and left.

To Jeanne she said, "Time to go. This is now a private matter."

Jeanne slumped to her feet. "Damn. Before it even got good. I tried to tell him I didn't think his setup was a good idea." She snatched up her backpack. "Congratulations, boys. You got your man." She sauntered past them, punching Sebastian in the arm before walking down the hall, waving a hand over her head and saying, "Night."

Through all this Sebastian had stood, arms at his side, staring at Darcelle, his face expressionless, the giddy excitement of earlier completely gone.

"You"—she pointed at him—"bedroom."

His gaze heated, but he strode out without a verbal response.

Darcelle watched him depart and then turned to Cade. "Take your time. The room is yours." Then she too went, presumably to chew on Sebastian, who seemed to accept the dressing down he was about to receive. But if Cade knew Sebastian, his boss would only take so much.

In the silence that now surrounded them, Bassinae tipped her head and met Cade's gaze, her face damp. "I was so afraid I would lose you."

He wiped a thumb over her cheek. He would have given anything for her not to endure what happened tonight, let alone watch the live vid from the cameras Jeanne had set in place. "I know. It had to be done."

"It's just..." She broke off, unable to continue.

He brushed her dreads back and cradled her head between his hands. "I was afraid too. If he figured out how much I care for you, he might think the best revenge was killing you. I couldn't let it get to that point. I couldn't put everyone in danger from this maniac, and that's the way it would have been. Even if I left, he might come after you for information."

He skimmed his mouth across hers, the softness of her lips sending tendrils of desire slipping along his nerve endings. If only that brilliant smile would flash onto her face, but it was unfair of him to expect her to be happy he was alive without also working through the emotional hit she'd taken tonight. He rested his lips against her forehead and waited for her to speak, to tell him whatever she needed to say. For now he would hold her, wrap her in the security of his arms until she was ready to release him.

Hesitantly she said, "I couldn't watch. Jeanne and Darcelle did. They told me what was happening, but there was no way I was going to witness you getting shot." Her palm stroked his back, up and then down, pausing and then repeating the journey. If he'd been the lion she always claimed he was, he would have been purring. Having looked death straight in the eye, this simple act more than anything let him appreciate he was still alive.

"Jeanne said he pointed a missile at you." She pulled away to look up at him, gripping his sides tightly. "A missile!"

He winced. "Yeah. Tonight didn't go quite like we expected, but it's over, and we got him. He's dead. And even if I hadn't killed him, the mob he's with would have. They're going to get a lot of scrutiny. Everyone knows they traffic in illegal weapons, but to have one waved around in the open... They aren't gonna be happy about that."

Her fingers dug in harder. "They wouldn't come after you too?"

A stab of pain shot through him. He brushed his knuckles across her cheek, looking deeply into her eyes. He wanted all fear for his safety to be erased from her mind. "No, Nordgren was working this offside. They don't have a beef against me. It's over." He released her and took her hand. "Now no more of this. Let's go home. I promised myself I'd fuck you until I couldn't move." A slow, taunting smile spread on his lips, and he raised his eyebrows at her. "You're not going to make me break my promise, are you?"

She snorted and answered him with a smirk, allowing him to pull her along out the penthouse entrance to the elevator that would take them to their own level. Inside he backed her against the wall, hands on either side of her head, and took her mouth in an unhurried, heated kiss that promised them both more to come.

* * * *

The chime pinged. He scooped her into his arms and carried her to his apartment, moving toward it in long strides, his impassioned hazel gaze riveted on her face. The ease with which he bore her weight sent a prickle of panic running through Bassinae. She mentally reprimanded herself. That was a reaction predicated on her past, not her now or her future. His powerful physique was used to protect.

The carnal hunger flickering in his eyes triggered a response in her that was nothing like fear, a craving that could only be satisfied by him deep inside her, filling her, connecting them in a primal act of bonding. To her dismay he paused outside his door before entering, but then his words melted her.

"You are the best thing in my life. And not just because you've got the most fuckable body I've ever seen. But damn, woman, we're not leaving this apartment until I've taken you every way known to man." His lips claimed hers, and his tongue pressed, demanding entrance, which she ceded, moaning. He plundered her mouth with an urgency that might have overwhelmed her in the past. Now it ramped up the desire building inside her. Her nipples were taut, aching for his fingers to pluck them. She needed his hands smoothing over her skin, grasping her tight against him, but not out here where the others living on this level could step out and observe them.

He groaned when she moved back from the kiss and asked him, "Why are we still in the corridor?"

His nostrils flared. "Because I can't think when you're in my arms." The next instant she was on the floor standing next to him while he unlocked the door and flung it open. Then she was once again being carried. He pushed the door shut with the sole of his boot and headed toward his bedroom, kicking a box out of his path.

The bed was neatly made, the room almost military in its sparseness. But that didn't mean Cade didn't like his luxuries. When he placed her in the center of the mattress, the soft support was like a miracle to muscles that had been tight with tension all night. She sighed and raised her arms over her head, stretching. He dropped to the bed, one knee beside her, his hands on either side of her, gazing at her. "You're going to come so many times you lose count before I'm done with you."

Bassinae lifted her torso to catch hold around his neck and pull him to her. But he pushed himself away and got to his feet, peeling off his shirt, yanking his boots and socks off, and stripping off his pants until he was nude. How many massages had she given him, her hands sliding over his muscular physique and fingers kneading the tantalizing golden brown of his skin? Tonight, rather than search for knots to work out, she would seek the places on him that made him shudder in erotic pleasure. His cock jutted from its nest of dark blonde curls. He stood as though poised at the starting line of a long-distance race, fists clenched in an attempt to temper his eagerness and not surge forward, setting a pace for a dash, not the marathon he had said he planned.

She watched him, her mind a heady mix of thoughts, lusty and wicked. Her bad girl wasn't going to give him a break. She intended to bring it hot and relentless. Her movements sensuous, she sat and scooted to the end of the bed, making him swallow hard. "You're not the only one who's going to be doing the fucking here." She dragged her fingers up his erection.

His hands landed on her shoulders, his thumbs caressing her skin in circles. "Gods, woman. Suck my cock. I've been dreaming about your lips around it, taking me in, swirling your tongue...oh shit. Yeah, just like that."

It was probably the one time he wouldn't appreciate her smiling, but she did it anyway, releasing the suction she'd applied as she'd slid her mouth over his shaft. "Like this?" She repeated the motion.

"Yeah...yeah...that's..."

She lifted her eyes to glimpse his face as she pulled back toward his tip. His gaze was riveted on the point where they were joined, his breathing increasing and his fingers tightening on her shoulders. She plunged again, stroking the underside of his erection with her tongue, and he grew harder.

His hands fumbled to grasp her head. "I can't take much more of this. You'll make me come if you don't stop."

"Mmmm." She slipped him from her mouth and nibbled a path to his balls, giving each a swirl.

"Oh fuck."

This is one way to have a man by his balls. She giggled wickedly to herself and gave a lick to his sac, drawing a line between the globes within and fluffing them in her hand while she pulled away to grin at him.

"Minx." He lifted her under her arms and flung her back to the center of the bed, her laughter ending in a puff of air when she hit the mattress and sank into it. Without any wasted movements he stripped her, expertly unhooking, unbuttoning, and unzipping her garments.

When she was nude, he slid up her body. Now he would take her, manhandling her in the very best way. And she was ready for it, more than ready. An insatiable greediness was running rampant along her nerves, sending pulses of arousal to her nipples and clit. Her core muscles tightened. Her hips lifted in a demand that he fill her. Instead he rolled them over until she lay atop him, her fingers free to stroke the planes and ridges of his body. He cupped her head between his palms and pulled her to him, kissing her with reckless abandon, consuming her and stealing her breath. His mouth still pressed to her, he said, "Ride me."

She leaned back to study him. A slender ring of hazel edged in brown circled dilated pupils, dark wells brimming with passion. His chest rose and fell with each harsh inhale he took, pressing against her breasts, stimulating already sensitized nipples. His lips, those beautiful, generous lips, were parted, awaiting her response before he once again used them to impel her body to a higher plane of ecstasy.

Hands on his shoulders, she pushed herself up to straddle him, easing her way down his body until his rigid length pressed against her pussy. She rubbed her labia along him, watching him and enjoying the power she had to arouse and please him. He growled, proving she was driving him crazy. That she could do that, that he allowed her to control their lovemaking, made confidence roar through her. He'd said she had the most fuckable body he'd ever seen, and right here, right now she knew with absolute certainty it was true. It was gloriously, wonderfully true. She tipped her head back, exultation rushing through her, and smiled, elation stretching her lips more broadly than ever before.

When she dropped her chin and leveled that smile on Cade, his whole face suffused with a matching expression, one she'd never seen on him. Her heart ached seeing him radiate the same joy.

His voice gruff, he said, "You are so beautiful." But in mere moments his gaze turned lascivious. "And hot as hell. Ride me, woman, before I take matters into my own hands."

She pinched his nipple. "Not on your life." An impish impulse made her take her time. After sliding back, she stroked his erection base to tip several times until he growled at her. The smirk left her lips when she impaled herself on him, turning to a smile of hazy satisfaction, her eyes closing. The downward stroke had rubbed a spot inside her that strummed a note of pleasure, different but equally erotic as the one her clit produced when thumbed. The waves streamed to her fingertips.

Two large, warm hands clamped onto her hips, urging her to move. She began slowly but soon increased her rhythm until she was truly riding him, rocking from side to side as she moved up and down. His pelvis rose to grind into her. Her eyes flew open on a bright ping of pleasure. He was watching her, his eyes lit with desire, his lips parted, the patch of golden-brown, wiry hair nestled between his nipples rising and falling with every breath he took. He was hers. Completely. She reached behind her, seeking between his thighs, which he widened to assist her exploration. When her fingers found his balls, she stroked them.

"Don't stop. Whatever you do, don't stop."

The rasp of his voice was like flint to dried tinder, lighting a conflagration inside her. *As if I could. Not even possible.*

He cupped her breasts, plucking at the nipples with his thumbs and forefingers before dropping one hand to where they were joined to press a finger to her clit, letting the movement of their bodies create the rub that sent her soaring into an explosive climax. She rode it out as he sat, clamping his arms around her, holding her tightly against his groin, coming in deep surges punctuated by murmurs of filthy appreciation.

✳ ✳ ✳ ✳

It was 11:18 the next day when Cade woke after a night of lovemaking with Bassinae, not exactly rested but invigorated nevertheless. He nudged Bassinae, who was sprawled on her side next to him, deeply sunken in slumber. "Morning, Miss Mary. Time to rise and shine."

She swiped her hand toward him and mumbled, "Go away. Need to sleep."

He chuckled and nuzzled his face into her nape. "Okay. I'll be back."

"Hmmm. Promise?"

"Promise," he whispered, kissing her below her ear.

A half hour later he was showered, dressed, and bopping along the hall, the latest reggae love song playing on a loop in his mind. He made his way to Max's office, finding the older man sitting behind his desk, looking as dapper as Cade had ever seen him.

"Whoa, Max. You got a date or a date in court?"

Max lifted his gaze, narrowing his eyes in a basilisk stare at Cade. "Neither. I am meeting someone. It is not a date. And it is none of your business."

Cade yanked one of the side chairs away from the wall, turned it, and straddled the seat facing Sebastian St. Croix's man of affairs. "Point taken. I'm here to report for duty. Am I still on to do recon for the Bernard place?"

"Yes, you are. However, we planned to give you the day off."

Cade grinned. "Not necessary. Bassinae is down for the count, so I'm yours in the meantime."

The look of disdain Max sent him made Cade broaden his grin.

"I do not need to be regaled with announcements of your achievements with the young lady. I get quite enough of that from other sources." Max dropped his gaze to the vidscreen embedded in his desk.

Whoever he was meeting, it was evident Max wasn't happy about the prospect. He could be gruff and put a drill sergeant to shame when chewing someone out, but he was rarely if ever cranky.

Without looking up, he said, "Go see Jeanne. She'll set you up with the necessary gear. Standard scope of discovery."

Huh. It appeared even the supremely self-contained and disciplined Max, whom Cade saw as a mentor, didn't always have his shit together. "You need to talk, I'll listen. Can't promise you any good advice."

The suggestion was rejected in a brisk, no-nonsense manner. "No, thank you." He paused and looked directly at Cade. "I appreciate the offer." Then he returned his attention to what he'd been working on at his desk.

"Right." *I tried.* Cade stood, twirling the chair and returning it to its spot along the wall. "I'm off to see Jeanne." He rubbed his stomach. "I'll have to eat three triple deluxe burgers to make up for all the energy I used last night." When no response came, he glanced at Max under his eyebrows. "In bed."

Max plucked a hard candy from the bowl he kept on his desk and threw it at Cade. "Out of here, you oversexed lummox."

The candy hit Cade in the arm he lifted to shield himself. A hint of a smile played around Max's lips. Cade turned and sauntered out the door. Now that he had brightened Max's day, it was Jeanne's turn.

He found her sorting through a pile of vid cameras. "Hey, gorgeous, I'm still waiting on the green."

When she lifted her gaze to him, her expression was puzzled until he grasped a hunk of his hair and gave her a meaningful look. "Oh. I haven't had time. Putting up cameras. Taking down cameras. Try not to get any more deranged murderers stalking you. It puts a crimp in my beauty regimen."

"I'll make a note of that. Do not make bad men mad at you." He pointed his finger at his temple, pretending it was a gun, and fired. He got no reaction.

"Why are you here? I wasn't expecting you until tomorrow."

He flashed a lecherous grin. "Bassinae needs her rest. So I came by today to get started on the Bernard thing."

Jeanne ignored the bait, continuing to check camera tags and comparing them to the info on her vidscreen. "Lucky for you I already have the gear you need packed in a ready bag. The one with the blue tag on the shelf. Tablet's got the datasheets on it. I gave you a set of surveillance glasses and a handheld vid camera as back up. Take the silver coupe. It's just been serviced."

"Snacks?" He slid sideways through the narrow gap between her work table and the wall, picking up the satchel and perching it on the corner of her table to check inside.

"Three water bottles and a couple of peanut butter and jelly sandwiches."

"If the way to a man's heart is through his stomach, you're never gonna find love." He cinched the bag closed again. "I'll stop for more."

Jeanne set the camera in her hand down and turned toward him. "If it weren't for that damn panic room, this would be an easy job. Sebastian's going to have to figure out another way to get into it. It's state-of-the-art, never been cracked. I've gotten my hands on the schematics, but the multiple biometric security measures are impossible to get past without some major equipment and days to work on it. I don't see that happening for us."

"He'll figure something out. He always does." Cade slung the ready bag over his shoulder.

She bit her lip and nodded. "Let's hope it's safer than the last thing he came up with. At least today you shouldn't have any problems. No missiles, anyway."

"Yeah. Last night rates a category all its own."

"I gotta say. I nearly crapped my pants, and I wasn't even there." She ducked her head. "Thanks for saving my big brother and Max."

Cade turned his head toward the door. "Yeah. Training kicked in. You don't think. You do."

They looked at one another, Cade seeing the sincerity in her eyes. "Whatever. You did what needed doing when it needed doing. I admire that." Then she scowled and pointed a finger at him. "But don't for a second think I'll ever admit that in front of someone else."

He grinned and blew her a kiss. "I love you, too."

The love song tapping its accented offbeat in his head, he left her with a smirk on his face. Sebastian would come up with a workable plan for this job. Breaking and entering was his specialty, after all. And Darcelle would be on the ground, deeply involved. That alone would make Sebastian cautious. Last night she had probably been just as angry at Sebastian's initial reaction after the shooting as she had been at the possibility they might have been killed.

Maybe he should explain that excitement after a traumatic event was a response some people had. It might not seem as logical or sensitive as others like anger, disbelief, or numbness, but it happened to the best of people, including, apparently, Sebastian. Far more important in Cade's mind, the man didn't run away. Yeah, last night's events would temper Sebastian's belief in his infallibility, which was all to the good.

CHAPTER EIGHT

FIVE DAYS AFTER the nearly catastrophic night that ended the threat to Cade, Bassinae rushed to change from her exercise clothes to jeans and a T-shirt. She was running late, having spent an extra half hour talking with a self-defense student who was having a problem taking any aggressive actions. The woman's arrival at Do It Now hadn't been her own decision, but one made by protective services when she was discovered in a cage during an illegal substance raid at a compound outside the city. Caught between the indoctrination that still compromised her emotional well-being and the center's insistence she learn to defend herself, the woman had been in tears. Bassinae had acknowledged her struggle and told her she would place her in another class that moved at a slower pace. They'd parted with a hug.

Each individual's path out of abuse was different. Do It Now wasn't a cookie-cutter program, so Bassinae expected days that ran long. She was happy to put in the extra time because the same had been done for her. But at the moment she needed to trot to make it to the meeting Sebastian had called. She was ready to present her plan for the Bernard job, or as Sebastian was now calling it, the Pharaoh's jewels heist.

She slipped into her seat at the conference table as Sebastian entered the room, followed by Darcelle. Cade leaned toward Bassinae for a quick kiss, which Bassinae extended by sliding her fingers around his neck and keeping him close.

When she finally released him, he asked, "How was your day?"

Bassinae smiled. "Good. I'll tell you later. And yours?"

He scooped her hand in his. "Always excellent when you're part of it."

Across from them Jeanne snorted. "Would you two like a little syrup to go with all that sweetness?"

Cade lifted Bassinae's fingers to his lips and said, "You're just jealous." Then he kissed them.

"I, for one, am glad Cade is still alive to be his charming self," Darcelle said, giving Sebastian a pointed glare.

He lowered his chin and leveled a heated stare at her. "I thought we'd settled that issue, but I'm willing to return to the discussion if that's what you want."

Darcelle's expression was sultry. "No talking. I'd much rather you'd spend more time making it up to me. But if a fight will energize you, I can manage that."

Sebastian gave her a wicked smile. "I don't think I'll be the one—"

A loud *thump* sounded. Max slapped his palm firmly on the table in front of him and said, "Children, can we please get down to business. I have more important things to do than listen to you flirt or snipe at one another."

In unison they all turned to look at Max, who was scowling, seeming more like a curmudgeon than his normal implacable self.

Sebastian straightened in his seat. "My apologies. I'll try to make this quick so everyone can get to their suppers. Cade has done his usual excellent job over the last few days surveilling the grounds and the house's exterior as well as the comings and goings of the occupants. Bernard has only two human staff, a cook and his personal assistant, who also acts as his driver. Both are live-in. Cleaning and maintenance is handled by house droids. Bassinae, I asked you to come up with ideas for how we proceed. What have you got?"

She straightened in her seat. "I assumed, as we probably all did, that this would be a fairly easy task along the lines of previous heists. Darcelle and Sebastian do their magic and break into the mansion, cracking the safe and retrieving the jewelry. Plan the heist for when Bernard is out of town, and we probably wouldn't even need a distraction. We'd use two extraction positions with Max and Cade. But a problem has arisen, and I'm not sure how we'll handle it other than I imagine it will be something Jeanne would have to do."

Sebastian tipped his head toward Bassinae. "Thank you. That's my assessment of the situation, too. Slipping into and out of the mansion won't be a problem. Where we encounter a block—and it's a sizable one—is the panic room security. The safe where Ms. Bernard believes the jewels are being kept is in that room, accessible only by Bernard. It's a new system that hasn't been broken. Jeanne is working on it, but it's not just layers that can be peeled away one by one. The process of unlocking it involves interwoven threads of multiple biometric and cryptographic measures. We won't be breaking in.

"The question then becomes how we get through that door. If you can't crack the system, you change the system. I propose we take a page from Mr. Nordgren's playbook."

A general stir went around the table at that statement.

Sebastian waved a hand in the air. "I understand he's not the best person for us to pattern ourselves after, but he got one thing right. He knew what Cade was up to because he compromised Cade's internal comm. I propose we do the same to Bernard's panic room intrusion system."

Max raised a finger. "You don't expect him to accept a message that his system needs upgrading without verifying with the company, do you?"

"No." He gave an apologetic look to Cade. "I don't expect him to be a sucker. He's too hard-nosed for that. No. We're going to make him come to us. Jeanne has said she can force the system to broadcast a false alarm. After several unnecessary alerts, Bernard will be comming the company to have the problem fixed. Before that happens we'll add a forwarding loop to his home and office comms. It will tag and send any calls directed to the panic room company to Jeanne. She'll schedule a date to have the system repaired."

"And what if Bernard uses his internal comm?" Max looked to Jeanne for the answer to his question.

She smirked. "Someone will get the delightful task of introducing a nanite carrying a bug that will do the same for his internal comm. Easy peasy with a microneedle. I suggest a slap to his face, although you don't have to worry about him feeling it, so you could do it with a handshake." She curled her lip. "But who wants to shake hands with that filth? I'll also include a self-destruct that I can initiate once we finish the job."

Gods, it would be cathartic to punish the creep. "May I be the one to stab him with the needle?" Bassinae bared her teeth in a fierce grin.

Cade looked at her, an eyebrow raised. "Miss Mary, you're scaring me."

She batted a hand at him. "I'd like to see this bastard pay for the way he treated Georgia."

When Cade scooted his chair closer to her and put his hand around her shoulders, she laid her cheek on his arm. He kissed the top of her head and said, "I know. I understand."

Sebastian focused his gaze on Bassinae. "We all understand, but you won't be doing the tagging. We'll get my mother to do that job. Can you convince her that she'd have an easier time gaining access to Bernard than you would? I'm sure she would love to slap him; doing it in public would be a bonus. And no one would ever believe she was injecting him with illicit nanites."

"Oh, she would. She most definitely would." Bassinae nodded. "Yeah, I think your mom and I can come up with a plan." Maybe she could also get Adele St. Croix to tell Sebastian she knew all about his cat burglar career. *It would make matters easier and eliminate my guilt for lying to Sebastian.*

"Good. I'm going to send in a team posing as maintenance techs for the company that sold Bernard the panic room. Bernard shouldn't recognize Jeanne." He grinned at his sister. "She was never much of a society party girl, and I doubt he hangs out in her normal haunts."

Jeanne smirked. "Yeah, me and evening gowns never got a long."

He turned his gaze to Bassinae. "I want you to be the second member of that team."

"Wait. What?" Cade pulled his arm from around Bassinae. "I should do that. I can handle the trouble that will follow if we're caught. I don't want her mixed up in that."

Sebastian sent Cade a look of sympathy. "I get it, Cade. I really do." He reached out and stroked the hand Darcelle rested on the table. "But it's not up to you. It's Bassinae's decision. And it's something I believe she's ready for. Jeanne will have her thoroughly prepared to handle any questions Hugo might ask and the steps for her part in the upgrade procedure. She's played minor roles with you before. This will be the next step up from that. Darcelle and I discussed it. We think she can do it."

Gritting his teeth, Cade crossed his arms over his chest. "I know she can do it. But this would be a felony if we're caught. That's serious."

"Again. That's not your decision to make. It's Bassinae's." Sebastian's gaze was pointed, his voice stern.

Bassinae wanted to wrap her arms around Cade's neck and kiss him. He could be bossy and overprotective, but it both warmed her heart and heated her blood that he cared so strongly for her. Instead she placed a palm on his shoulder, and said, "I'll do it."

When his head snapped toward her, she moved her hand to his forearm and stroked it. In a soothing tone of voice she said, "I understand the risks, but I also believe in what we're doing. And I trust Sebastian to make this work. Thank you for worrying about me, but I'm a big girl, and I've learned to be tough."

His lips pressed in a thin line, Cade tilted his head, remaining silent as he gazed into her eyes. Bassinae held her breath. She hadn't thought they'd reach such a critical juncture in their newly established relationship this soon. Would Cade reject the new, more independent person she was stretching to become, would he move past his own fears to back her, or would he acquiesce but only for the moment?

He uncrossed his arms and drew his thumb over her cheek. "I hate the idea of you being hurt or locked up. Prison is no place for Miss Mary. But I'll support you and do everything I can to help you as long as you agree to allow me to protect you to the best of my ability." His eyes blazed with a fierceness that asserted he meant every word.

"It's a deal." She smiled softly at him.

He wrapped a hand around her nape, pulled her to him, and gave her a thorough and very dominating kiss, overloading her senses with pleasure. Someone cleared his throat. Cade didn't allow that to interrupt him.

"Ahem."

Finally Cade broke their embrace, staring at her as he relaxed into his chair. Bassinae's face heated. She dropped her gaze to the tabletop.

She was relieved no awkward scuffing of feet occurred from the others. Sebastian resumed where he had left off. "That's settled then. Jeanne and Bassinae will handle the upgrade to the panic room security system. Once that's been accomplished, Darcelle and I will do a standard break-in, enter the panic room, open the safe, and steal the jewels. We'll reset the security system, remove any evidence of tampering, and make our escape. Max. Cade. I'll want you in separate locations to pick us up afterward. I'll give you the exact spots once Darcelle and I finish our plans for the burglary."

✶ ✶ ✶ ✶

Bassinae struggled not to fall behind. The three-inch, bright-red heels on her feet were difficult to manage. She hadn't worn anything this tall since she eliminated this type of footwear from her life when she'd moved on from Jessil. The heat in Cade's eyes the other day when she'd met him for lunch in a swingy dotted dress and matching high heels had sealed the deal. When she wasn't at work, she was dressing like a woman who enjoyed her own sex appeal. But keeping up with the long strides of Adele St. Croix took effort.

Sweeping through the hall of statues that led to Sebastian and Darcelle's private penthouse entrance, Adele said, "Let me do the talking. I know how to handle my son."

"Yes, ma'am." Bassinae had been commanded to call Sebastian's mother Adele, but at this moment when the woman was in full-throttle doyenne-of-the-upper-class mode, Bassinae felt their distinctions in rank acutely. Adele was the general, while she was a lowly lieutenant.

To Bassinae's surprise, Adele entered the penthouse without ringing. Was the passcode she used one Sebastian had given her, or had she obtained it from someone else? Then Bassinae remembered that Adele had done the interior design for the apartment.

They had made it to the end of the entry hall when Max met them. "Mrs. St. Croix. Bassinae." He nodded at her but returned his focus to Adele, recognizing who was the instigator of this unexpected visit. "Does Sebastian or Darcelle know you were coming?"

"No, Max. They do not. Something came up while I was lunching with Bassinae, and I must speak with my son immediately."

Max didn't allow his curiosity to show on his face. "It may take a few minutes for him to come to you. May I offer you refreshments on the main terrace? It's a beautiful day, and I believe we have a mating pair of Genevan finches building a nest under the eaves."

Adele looked down her nose at him. "Tell my son to get out of bed. Really! Half the day is gone already. He's become extremely lax since he met Darcelle. I can only hope this means we'll have a grandchild in the offing." She waved a hand at Max. "Go on. We'll find our own way to the terrace. Tea for me. And you, my dear?" She directed the question to Bassinae.

"Yes, ma'am."

Adele nodded. "Coffee for Sebastian. And whatever Darcelle prefers in the morning. I'm sure she'll accompany him." Then she strode off, the green of the gauzy wrap she wore over an even darker sheath floating back in a cloud behind her. "Come."

Once again Bassinae strove to keep pace with Adele. The main terrace was a gorgeous space. It beat her small balcony by miles. Adele settled herself in the center of an outdoor divan and patted the spot beside her. "Sit by me, dear."

Finches were indeed building a nest under the eaves on the far side of the terrace. They were retrieving long dried grasses from a pile in the corner. The plantings out here were too well-kept to provide that much material. Someone had put it there to encourage nest building, but who? Darcelle? Max? Surely not Sebastian.

Their tea arrived a few minutes before Sebastian and Darcelle. Bassinae was taking her first sip when Sebastian spoke. "Mother. How wonderful for you to drop by." He walked to her and bent to kiss her cheek before settling into the arm chair directly across from Adele. Both he and Darcelle were dressed in casual clothing, looking like they planned to share a quiet weekend with one another.

"Morning, Adele." Darcelle sat in the wicker rocker beside Bassinae. "Hey. Love the outfit. It's going good with Cade? Don't answer. I can see it is."

Meanwhile, Sebastian and Adele exchanged polite conversation about the weather. Bassinae wondered how long it would take Adele to get around to the reason they had come.

"You've recruited a mated pair of finches." Adele pointed to the nest. "I didn't know you still did that."

Sebastian turned and looked over his shoulder, smiling. "I haven't in years." He brought his gaze to Darcelle, the expression remaining on his face when he said, "Someone inspires me to enjoy the beauty in life again." Darcelle winked at him, and his lips spread into a wide grin.

A look of satisfaction filled Adele's face before she grew solemn. "I have something to tell you that may upset you."

Sebastian crossed his legs, leaning back, looking fully at ease. "I'm sure I can handle whatever it is."

"I know all about your clandestine activities."

To Sebastian's credit he didn't appear startled. "That sounds nefarious."

"Not quite the right word, but most definitely illicit. When we got Cheyenne back, Jeanne spilled the beans. I should say, I pried it out of her. She's not as good a liar as you are."

The corners of Sebastian's mouth turned up in a fake smile. "So you learned about the kidnapping."

Adele lifted her chin. "I heard a great deal more than that. You're a cat burglar, dear. You steal art and precious artifacts from the greedy collectors who buy them knowing they are dealing with stolen goods. I'm inordinately proud of you."

Sebastian's reaction went from two rapid blinks of his eyelids, followed by clearing his throat, and then furrowing his eyebrows. "I see."

Adele sighed and tapped the arm of the divan. "I've always believed you were the perfect blend between your father and me. You get your honor and duty from him. Gerald is great believer in the letter of the law, and you strive to emulate him. But strict adherence to legalities doesn't assure justice. Your tender heart for those in trouble comes from me. That and I raised you to believe our cultural heritage should belong to all, not just the few who can afford to have it on their walls or on their shelves. Your father wouldn't understand what you do, so we won't tell him. It would only lead to heartache. I, however, support what you're doing. I think it's admirable."

His eyebrows raised, Sebastian looked at Darcelle. In the stillness that extended until it was uncomfortable, Bassinae's body tensed. It wouldn't take Sebastian long to wonder about her role in this revelation.

Darcelle finally spoke. "We both acknowledge you would never willingly harm Sebastian, so we trust you'll say nothing of his activities to any other person."

"Certainly not." Adele's spine stiffened enough for the others to notice. "The less I'm told the better. I want no specifics."

"But you were the one who brought the Hugo Bernard job to us." Sebastian directed the question to his mother while arching an eyebrow at Bassinae.

"Yes. I approached Bassinae because I didn't want you to know I was aware of your activities. I didn't want to worry you, but this dear girl"—she laid a hand on Bassinae's arm—"convinced me otherwise."

Bassinae's response was much the same as a mouse caught out in the open by the cat when Sebastian's gaze settled on her. She froze. "I'm not pleased that you lied to me. That you allowed me to continue to assume that my mother was unaware of my extracurricular career. I'll grant you extenuating circumstances, since you've come forward and fixed the situation. But if you ever lie again like this, you will no longer be a member of this team. Do you understand?"

Bassinae nodded and then slumped in relief, dropping her gaze to her lap where her fingers lay tightly entwined.

"Don't scare the poor girl," Adele said patting Bassinae's arm. "She was caught between us. And she tells me you require my assistance in retrieving Georgia's jewelry. I'm only too happy to do anything I can. I've been told someone must slap Hugo. And that I'm not only happy to do but ecstatically delighted to do. I need the details of how and when."

Once the conversation was no longer focused on her, Bassinae brought her gaze back to watching the exchange between mother and son, relieved that she had gotten off so lightly. Steeling herself for the next revelation she had to make, she tightened her fists and waited for a chance to speak.

Sebastian briefly closed his eyes, but by the time his mother finished speaking, he was once again looking at her, his expression neutral. "When? As soon as possible. How? Jeanne will provide the microneedle with the nanites we need in Hugo's system. She'll explain everything to you. Since I'm certain you'll warn her I've learned of her slip of the tongue, you may tell her I will speak with her later." He rose from his chair. "I intend to spend the weekend with my wife. Alone."

"Sir." Bassinae resisted the urge to squirm when all three pairs of eyes focused on her. "Yesterday, Georgia asked to be included in the plan to steal the jewelry."

"No. Tell her that's impossible. You should have already made that clear." Sebastian bent and kissed his mother.

"I had an idea of how we could use her as a distraction. Sort of like you've used me in the past." Sebastian was shaking his head, so she hurried through her reasons. "This would be so good for her. To be able to deal a personal blow, to get back some of the power she's always ceded to her husband. It won't really change the plan much. You were planning for Jeanne to distract the security droid by having the mansion's security system ping an alert as far away as possible from your actual point of entry. I think with Georgia's help I can provide an even better diversion." Despite her intention to maintain a confident appearance, she winced at the thundercloud of Sebastian's face when she finished.

"That's an excellent idea."

Sebastian looked at his wife, his eyes narrowing when she cocked an eyebrow at him.

"Yes. It would be the best thing in the world for Georgia. If you could manage something that included her even in the smallest way, I'd be ever so grateful," Adele said.

Sebastian sighed and crossed his arms over his chest. "Fine. I'll listen to your idea. But it will wait until after this weekend is over. The merger I've been working on has gone through. I'm exhausted and ready for some rest."

Darcelle kicked Bassinae with the toe of her shoe to get her attention. Then she winked. Bassinae acknowledged her with a weak smile.

After Sebastian led Darcelle from the terrace, Adele took a long sip from her cup. "Let's finish our tea, and then we'll go find Jeanne."

CHAPTER NINE

BASSINAE STOOD NEXT to Jeanne in the foyer to the Bernard mansion, hoping that her body language didn't give away the nerves that were making her heart beat a fraction too quickly and her stomach fill with a flight of butterflies. Jeanne didn't look calm, but neither did she appear nervous. She impatiently tapped her fingers on the side of the tech bag she had slung over her shoulder as though waiting for the owner of the house to come escort them to the panic room was an imposition on her time.

What they had seen of the mansion so far made Bassinae imagine they were requesting an audience with a duke or count or maybe even a prince. Pale blue and ivory were the main colors with an abundance of gold in the fanciful moldings that twined and curved from the ceiling and down the walls. The furnishings were equally intricate, the coverings of chairs and divans in florals and leafy themes that matched the color scheme. It was like a fairy court. Bassinae loved it and felt completely underdressed.

She and Jeanne wore Overscheim Security service uniforms, atrocious pale green coveralls, and caps. Jeanne also sported a pair of magnification glasses with the lens piece popped up so she could peer at the droid who'd answered the door and pinged Hugo Bernard that he had guests. That had been five minutes ago. Five minutes in which the droid, designed to look like a gray-haired male butler, stood, hands folded between them and the rest of the mansion.

"Is he coming? We don't have all day. This was a scheduled appointment," Jeanne snapped.

The droid had been programmed with an old-French accent, which sounded odd considering they were speaking Standard but entirely in keeping with the decor. "The master has informed me he will be here momentarily. Perhaps you would like to take a seat while you wait." He gestured to the small sitting room to their left where a not particularly comfortable-looking ivory divan stood against one wall beneath an enormous mirror with an eight-inch-wide gilded frame. Under any other circumstances, Bassinae would have accepted, enjoying the opportunity to pretend she was a member of the aristocracy awaiting a rendezvous with a handsome, rakish prince who looked amazingly like Cade.

She mentally kicked herself, but at least the fantasy had helped calm her nerves. They weren't meeting prince charming. Quite the opposite. Hugo Bernard was a pig, and they were here to help his abused wife get some of hers back on the bastard.

Jeanne rejected the droid's offer with a blunt response. "No. Why don't you show us to the panic room? We can at least set up our equipment before Mr. Bernard comes to open it."

"I apologize, but that would be impossible. The master allows no one but myself and Mr. Fingle to enter his private domain."

"How much longer does he expect us to wait? He's not the only person on our schedule today. We have another client we're expected to fit in. We could be on our way to that job if Mr. Bernard has changed his mind about the urgency of his problem. I was told this was a top priority. I'll give him three more minutes; then we're leaving."

This didn't faze the droid in the least. Its face remained impassive. "I apologize. I assure you Mr. Bernard will come as quickly as possible. This is a highlighted appointment on his calendar."

A young fellow, tall and gangly, appeared around a corner. "It's all right, Francois. Mr. Bernard has sent me to escort them to his office."

The droid moved to the side to escape being bumped by the onrushing man. "As you say, Mr. Fingle."

Mr. Fingle, having loped to take the spot the droid had vacated, immediately turned on his heel, gestured them forward, and said, "Follow me."

The pace he set and the length of his legs made Bassinae trot to keep up, while Jeanne fell behind, refusing to be rushed. Continuing to speak with occasional glances over his shoulder to assure himself they still followed, he introduced himself as Mr. Fingle, Mr. Bernard's assistant. "I apologize for the delay. Mr. Bernard is most insistent that the problem with his panic room security be fixed as soon as possible."

Their path led up a flight of stairs, down hallways, until at last Fingle stopped outside a door that had its own palm-print security panel. The door unlocked after he placed his hand to it, and he stepped in, holding the knob for them to enter.

Hugo Bernard, a barrel-chested man, dressed in a finely tailored suit, stood looking out a window. He turned and scowled at them, inspecting each of them from head to toe.

Bassinae wondered if Bernard always looked annoyed. From Georgia's stories Bassinae had concluded he was peevish and self-involved. Although Georgia hadn't come right out and said that. No, she was still justifying many of the man's actions. That would change with therapy.

"That will be all, Fingle. And tell the damned cook never to put raisins in my oatmeal muffins again. I don't pay her to get creative."

"Yes. Sir." Fingle exited.

"Credentials. Let me see them now." The large, beefy hand Bernard held out to them was soft, as though he never did manual labor, which Bassinae was sure of before she glimpsed his uncalloused fingers.

Bassinae fumbled in her pocket for hers while Jeanne whipped hers out and sauntered toward him. She held her palm out to Bassinae for her card and then handed both to Bernard. He popped them each in turn into a reader slot in the massive mahogany desk that was the focal piece of the room. Satisfied that they were who they said they were, he gave them back to Jeanne.

The volume of his voice ratcheted up, his finger jabbing toward the panic room, Bernard said, "That damned thing has been setting off the alarm, waking me at ungodly hours, interrupting my dinner. I was promised this was the very best system on the market. I want it fixed. If it doesn't perform as expected after this, I'll want my money back and a competitor's system installed at your company's expense." He continued to glare at them.

"That's what we're here to do, Mr. Bernard." Jeanne let her weight shift to one leg, cocking her hip out. "If you'll unlock it, we'll get right to work."

Bernard bristled at Jeanne's tone and stance, but apparently thought better of admonishing her for her attitude. He marched to the panic room entrance. "Turn around."

Jeanne rolled her eyes before complying. Bassinae was happy to do whatever was necessary to get this over. Her heart was again beating rapidly, her stomach flutters replaced by twitchiness in her arms and legs.

"There you go. Make this as quick as possible. I'm a busy man." When Bassinae turned, the man's countenance matched the angry tone of his words. She realized it was probably the only expression Hugo Bernard ever held. An example of what her nana had claimed could happen if you never smiled. His face had frozen that way.

Jeanne strolled past him into the panic room. "Ain't we all." She went straight to the access panel, setting her tech bag on the floor below it. "Get set up while I open this," she said to Bassinae, ignoring Bernard, who stood in the door watching them. She pulled a pair of sterile plasti-gloves from the pack in her bag, offering it to Bassinae. Once they had the gloves on, they began.

Opening the case she'd been carrying, with her back to Bernard, Bassinae's skin crawled. She'd believed Georgia, but being in Hugo Bernard's presence confirmed everything she'd been told. He was a toad. No, that wasn't fair to toads. He was a troll who had somehow escaped from under his bridge to this mansion and, instead of enjoying his success, continued to harass anyone who came near him.

"Why did they send two of you? So they can charge me double?"

Jeanne snorted. "Explain things to the man."

Damn Jeanne. Bassinae focused on the items she was laying out on the floor; most she had no clue as to their use. "It's for your protection, sir. One tech might be bought off to compromise your system, but two is less likely. We're randomly paired each day. So we never know what job we'll be assigned or who we'll be working with. Again for your protection, sir. Overscheim takes every precaution for their clients. This service call is free. Anytime your system needs attention, we're happy to provide whatever is necessary."

"Damn well should for the prices they charge."

"Here." Jeanne handed her a silicone card. "Let me have the spray." She blew a blast of air into the mechanism and flipped the lenses of her glasses in place, peering into the guts of the security panel. "It looks good in here. Must be a problem with the card. We're replacing it and taking the used one. Our lab will examine it to determine what caused the trouble. They'll send you a report."

Bassinae took the can from her and handed her the new card. Once Jeanne popped it in place, she sealed the access panel. By the time she'd finished, Bassinae had her case repacked. She was ready to leave, happy she'd never have to set foot in this house again.

"Is that it? That's all you have to do?"

"Yep." She retrieved her bag from the floor, pulled out a plasti-coated card, and handed it to him. "You'll have to initialize the system again with your biometric data and passwords. The instructions are there. The same procedure you used before. I'm sure you'll want privacy for that." Jeanne said the last with an edge of snark to her tone.

He stepped out of the way so they could get past. "Francois, see them out."

The butler droid was standing against a wall in the office. He turned the knob and held the door for them to leave. Jeanne gave the droid a calculating look. "Awesome ninja moves there, Francois. I didn't even hear you come in."

"Thank you. Follow me, please."

Bassinae wished it were Fingle escorting them. Then they'd be out of the place faster. But Francois set a sedate pace, which allowed Jeanne to saunter and the jitters that had moved from Bassinae's limbs to her stomach to make a wreck of it. Not until they were in the van, emblazoned on both sides with the Overscheim Security logo, and Jeanne had driven the long drive to the mansion's gatehouse and passed through it, did Bassinae relax.

"That droid might be a problem. It's not just a butler. Probably a security droid, too. I'll let Sebastian know." She glanced at Bassinae. "You did good."

Bassinae smiled, covered her nose with her hands, and bent over. Laughter overwhelmed her, clear and bright. She had done well. She hadn't dropped anything or given them away. And if he had detected a tremor in her voice when she'd spoken to him, knowing Hugo Bernard, he would attribute that to the fear he inspired in mere mortals.

She sat up and grinned at Jeanne. "I want to do it again."

* * * *

Cade was ambivalent. He loved the delight Bassinae expressed at her successful role in subverting the security on Hugo Bernard's panic room. It was another step in becoming the confidant woman she was always meant to be. But he was annoyed that when she returned from the Bernard mansion, she joyously proclaimed that her expanded role in Sebastian's theft ring was the something missing in her life. Couldn't she see that it was the change in their relationship that was the big difference?

It was for him. He'd thought it was for her too, but now he wasn't sure. Maybe he was just another stepping stone on her path to becoming a new woman. Now that he thought about it, she'd turned on a dime after the shooting at the bank. One day she was *I'll never be involved with a man again* and the next *I love you, Cade.* And she'd been doped to the gills on pain meds the first time she said that. She'd never actually said the words since then. He had. Multiple times. But Bassinae hadn't. Had she moved from friend to friend with benefits?

Next to him she rolled to her side, still asleep. She was it for him. The woman. The one. *Fuck, I feel like such a girl. Tell me you love me forever and ever.* He palmed his face. Somehow, without rushing her—because that wouldn't go well—he was going to have to find a way to get her to understand that he was in this for the long-term, rocking chairs on the terrace when they were one hundred and three.

"What's wrong?" Voice drowsy, Bassinae peered at him.

"I've been thinking about us." He scooted to sit against the headboard, pulling the sheet up around his waist.

She pushed up with her elbow and propped her head on her palm. "Yeah. You don't look happy." She dropped her gaze to the top sheet and bunched it up over her breasts. "I thought this was working between us."

"It is. It's the best thing to ever happen to me." Their gazes lifted and met at the same moment.

"You don't look like it is."

He broke his gaze from hers and focused on his fingers clenched in the sheets. "I'm sorry." He pushed a hand through his hair. "If we're going to be together, we both need to be clear about..." *No no no no. Don't tell her you want to know where she sees this relationship going.* "I want to be totally open with you. There are parts of my past I haven't shared with you, and I think I should. We shouldn't have any secrets from one another."

Bassinae rubbed his knee with her hand. She probably hoped that action would comfort him.

Now that I claimed I have things to share with her, why does it suddenly feel like a big deal? I've told the story to Sebastian and discussed it in detail with Max. Hell, I even told Jeanne recently. *But telling Bassinae was making his stomach churn.* Suck it up. If you want her to be transparent with you, you have to be willing to take the first step.

"I need to tell you about Undoa Prime. I don't want you to wonder about my role in the atrocity."

She squeezed his thigh. "I know it wasn't your fault. That's all I need to know."

"I appreciate your trust, but I want you to know the details. We were on Undoa Prime to stop a rebellion. Half the time when Fleet dropped you on a planet, it was hard to tell which side was the good guys. You do what your commanders tell you to do. That's how it was on Undoa Prime. We did our job." The story of that last day down planet flowed out of him once he'd begun. Bassinae listened, rubbing his knee off and on.

"After that my career was pretty much shot. I accepted an honorable discharge and returned here to my home planet. I wasn't received with joy and acclamation, as you can imagine. No one wanted to hire me for what I was good at, security muscle, so I took the best job I could find, short-order cook."

Bassinae rolled to her back and gazed at him. "You can cook?"

He reached out and rubbed his thumb across her cheek. "Out of all that, you focus on the cooking?"

She smiled at him. "I didn't know you could cook. You eat out most of the time."

"I'm lazy."

She delicately snorted, scooted next to him, and wrapped her arm around him. "You're wonderful and brave. The kind of man who tries to do the right thing and broods about what he should have done better." She brought her gaze to his. "I love you, Cade Johnson, and nothing from your past is going to change that."

He broke eye contact to survey their surroundings before returning his focus to her, his expression solemn. "That's good. That's the first time you told me you love me since the clinic."

Pushing up on one hip, she looked at him with wide eyes. "Is that what's been bothering you?"

He ducked his head.

"It is." She slid on top of him, laying her head on his shoulder, the warmth of her body soothing him. "I love you. I think I have for a long time and didn't realize I needed you to be more than my best friend. You're right. Best friends don't share everything, but we're more than best friends. If we want what we're building between us to last, we have to be willing to put everything on the table."

Her words sent joy coursing through him. His heart rate kicked up. It wouldn't have surprised him if it had burst, it felt so full. He wrapped his arms tight around her and squeezed, nuzzling and kissing the top of her head. She gripped him tight in return and kissed his collarbone.

"My turn." He tried to keep her from sitting up, but she resisted his attempt to keep her tucked into his embrace and sat up cross-legged next to him. "I've never told you how I ended up in trouble. It's such a part of who I am, I can't believe I haven't told you before this."

She bit her lip and heaved a sigh. "I met Jessil when I was seventeen. He was older, handsome in a broody, bad-boy way. I fell for him. Not love. I know what that is now. He gave me a sense of worth that I suppose every young woman is looking for, especially if she grew up without a father. That's how the therapist explained it. Anyway, being with him made me feel special that I had captured his attention over all the other women he could have."

"At first I was thrilled by how he dominated all aspects of my life. Who I could see. Where I could go. He'd even tell me to change if he didn't like what I was wearing. As time passed, I slowly realized that he never complimented me. I was never good enough for him. He'd always been forceful and aggressive, especially during sex, but the slap to the butt turned from a playful pop to something more painful. I told myself if I did things his way, he'd stop. That I had to make myself into what he wanted or he would leave me.

"It got worse. He slammed me into walls, slapped my face, and threatened to let his buddies fuck me. I took it all until the day he punched me in the jaw. I don't even remember what made him mad. It could be something as silly as me sitting with my legs closed instead of apart so he could see my panties. I came to my senses in the hospital. They sent a therapist to my room to talk with me. She pointed out a few things that I was suppressing. I made up my mind that Jessil and I were over for good. When Sebastian found me, I was struggling to stay alive. I was afraid Jessil would find me, so I stayed away from my friends, most of whom hadn't been part of my life for a long time. I was determined not to go back to him."

His expression dark, Cade said, "Give me a last name, and I'll teach that cretin what happens to men who hit women."

"No." She placed a hand on his cheek. "You're not getting into trouble over that lowlife. I should have agreed to have him prosecuted. The hospital social worker arranged it with the police, but I was afraid he'd come after me for sure if I did. I just wanted to escape."

A muscle twitched in Cade's jaw. "I'm sorry you went through all that. You deserved better.

"So, did you flash that Miss Mary Sunshine smile at Sebastian? Is that what made him help you?"

Bassinae grinned. "No. I think it was because he saw me helping an elderly woman who dropped her package. An orange had rolled away, and I retrieved it for her. She went on her way, and I went back to where I'd left my sign. *Will work for food.* It was apparent to most people that I was hungry, but I gave her the fruit and treated her with kindness. What goes around comes around. It just came around really fast for me."

"That sounds like Sebastian. He sees things others miss, like the priceless jewel you are."

She batted her eyes at him. "So how about you? How'd Sebastian discover you?"

Cade ran a hand along her thigh. "A reporter wanted to do a story on the anniversary of the Undoa Prime atrocity. I was his local angle. Interviewed me. Brought my current circumstances into it. How I'd been as much a victim of the massacre as those that died." He glanced down at her. "Which I could have used when I arrived and was looking for a job." He rubbed a finger above his lips. "Sebastian saw it. Had Max comm me with an opportunity to work for him. I thought I'd be given an entry-level position in security in a company he owned, but it turned out he wanted me to be his personal security."

"That's when I met you." He gave a gentle tug on one of her dreads.

When she slid down beside him again, his groin hardened. It took only one stroke of her hand along his cock for him to pull her beneath him and claim her mouth.

CHAPTER TEN

THE DECISION WAS made to infiltrate the Bernard mansion when Hugo and his assistant were safely out of town, and it was four hours after sunset when the service droids and cook would be settled for the night in standby mode or sleeping. That left Francois as the only one who might detect the stray noises of Sebastian and Darcelle entering and moving through the house. Bassinae and Georgia took the steps to the front door, ready for their mission to divert the security droid. The cat burglar duo would use that distraction to climb to the second floor, break in through a window in the room next to Hugo's office, and take possession of Georgia's jewelry.

Her spine straight and shoulders back, Georgia flipped the security panel open and pressed her palm to it. Both she and Bassinae had agreed it would be a good idea for Georgia to switch off the security for the rest of the house, but Sebastian had said that the droid might reengage it right when he and Darcelle were entering. It would be better to bypass the window lock, spoofing the system to show it was still shut.

Striding through the door, Georgia waved a hand. "Welcome to my former home."

Awed again, Bassinae said, "It's like a fairy court."

"Looks can deceive." Georgia narrowed her eyes, surveying the foyer and the rooms off it with distaste. "I thought Hugo was prince charming when we married."

From down the main corridor, Francois appeared while Bassinae was closing the door. "Madam. An unexpected pleasure. Mr. Bernard has assured me you would come home but could not give a specific date."

"I'm not coming home, Francois. Several weeks ago Hugo informed me he would be away tonight, so I chose this opportunity to collect more of my things." She gestured to Bassinae, who had turned to face them. "I've brought a friend to assist me."

He bowed to Bassinae and said, "We've met before. You're one of the two women who repaired the security panel in Mr. Bernard's panic room." The droid eyed her as though evaluating whether she was a physical threat.

"That was me," Bassinae said.

The droid turned his gaze to Georgia. "I believe, madam, you are under the influence of a con artist. This young woman works for the company that provides security for the master's panic room, and I believe she is using her knowledge of the system for nefarious purposes. She is not someone Mr. Bernard would wish for you to associate with."

"Don't be ridiculous." Georgia removed her jacket and handed it to Francois. "I met her at Do It Now. She's a volunteer who's been helping me adjust to life away from Hugo. She's completely trustworthy."

"That may be, but this is quite suspicious. This type of person is known for inserting themselves into the lives of the unsuspecting, arranging matters for their own gain. Mr. Bernard would—"

"Oh, for heaven's sake. We're going to my rooms. I want to gather more clothing and some of my personal items. We won't be going anywhere near Hugo's precious office, much less that panic room he's never let me in. Now that we're divorcing, he's going to have to be more forthcoming about what he keeps locked up in there."

"Yes, madam, but—"

Georgia marched past him. "Come with me, dear. If I'm no longer obeying Hugo's dictates, I'm certainly not going to allow his butler to determine what I may and may not do in my own home. Francois, if you're so concerned, you can follow behind and keep an eye on us. Make sure I don't accidentally stop off in Hugo's rooms and take some of his underwear or socks."

The droid did just that with Georgia's jacket over one arm. Georgia took Bassinae's arm and leaned into her as they climbed the stairs to the second level. "The bedroom suites are all on the right side of the house." She raised her voice. "Far away from Hugo's office." She lowered it and said, "Mine is at the back of the house. It has its own private balcony that overlooks my rose garden. I shall miss those flowers."

Bassinae patted her hand. "You'll have fun planting a new one. Or who knows, maybe you'll win the house in the divorce."

"I would sell it. I can't imagine living here ever again." She dropped Bassinae's arm and swung open a broad door. "This is my domain. No, I mean, this was my domain." She swept into the bedroom. "The dressing room is this way." Over her shoulder she called to Francois, "Coming, Francois? Please make sure the criminal element I've allowed inside doesn't abscond with my fake diamonds. I treasure them so."

"Yes, madam. I do wish you would take the matter seriously. The master is not likely to—"

Georgia stopped and turned to stare at the droid. "Apparently I haven't made it clear. I don't give a fig for what Hugo does or does not want. Please do not mention him again in my hearing."

The droid bowed. "As you say, madam."

After that he didn't interfere as Georgia and Bassinae rifled Georgia's closet and dresser drawers, piling what they pulled onto the bed before returning for more. When Bassinae received the signal that Sebastian and Darcelle had completed the heist and were out of the mansion, she asked Georgia the question they'd prearranged to be the sign that it was time to go. "Didn't you want to pick up your perfume as well?"

Georgia grinned. "Yes, I do. Thank you for the reminder." Once she'd retrieved it and added it to the pile, she said to Francois, "Please have these things boxed up and sent to the Hotel St. James. I'm establishing residency there while I consider my future."

"Yes, madam."

The droid followed them back down the stairs to the foyer, where he assisted Georgia into her jacket. Once they were outside at end of the walk, the pair paused to hug and laugh. Then they headed toward where Cade awaited them in the luxury sedan Sebastian had purchased to replace the one that had been crushed.

Cade exited the vehicle and helped Georgia to climb in. Then he gave Bassinae a kiss that was equal parts relief and desire. "Darcelle and Sebastian are on their way back to the penthouse. How'd your end go? Any problems?"

"Just fine." Bassinae reached up to rub away the wrinkles on his forehead. "The security droid warned Georgia I might be a con artist. Wouldn't let me out of his sight. Worked like a charm." She laughed and gave him a quick buss before climbing into the car.

She turned to face Georgia in the back seat. "I'll bring you the jewelry tomorrow. Sebastian thinks it would be safer to keep it in the penthouse safe tonight."

* * * *

The elevator ride to the floor where Do It Now was located was brief, but still Cade found enough time to kiss Bassinae thoroughly. They both were aware security cameras were trained on them, but he wouldn't let something like that stop him. The moment the doors had closed, he had her against the wall, pale blue backpack and all. She wrapped her legs around him and tangled her tongue with his. The man tasted so damn good. And now that she'd taken to wearing dresses when not working, he had easy access to caress her thighs with rough, insistent fingers.

When the ping came, warning them they'd reached their destination, he had enough time to set her down, face the back of the elevator, and adjust his cock before the doors closed on him. The guard, who was always stationed outside the elevators on this level, gave them each a nod. Bassinae stopped.

"Hey, James."

"Miss Bassinae." He smiled shyly at her.

"How's it going today?"

He stuck his thumbs in his pockets. "Quiet morning. No new clients overnight."

"Mmm. Cade's with me. We won't be accessing the private areas."

"Of course." He straightened his stance. "I know you wouldn't break the rules."

"Thanks, James." To Cade she said, "Let's get settled in an interview room, and then I'll comm Georgia." She took Cade's hand and led him past the check-in desk, waving to the woman sitting behind it, and pulled him into a small room. The walls were a soothing green. Two sets of chairs stood across from one another at a table holding an arrangement of delicately hued flowers.

Cade pushed the door closed before turning, lifting her, and setting her on the table. His palm on the back of her head, he took up where they'd left off in the elevator. When he broke the kiss, Bassinae thumped him on the chest with her palms. "Not here. For so many reasons."

Backing off, he said, "Understood." He grasped her hand. "I'm going to ask Sebastian for a bigger apartment." He pressed his forehead against hers and gazed at her intently. "For the two of us. I want us to move in together. Will you?"

She narrowed her eyes. "It's a little soon."

"No, it's not. We've taken years to get to this point."

Her face relaxed, softly she said, "Yeah. Okay."

He lifted her from the floor, gave her a smacking kiss, and spun them around.

"Enough. Put me down. We have work to do."

Chuckling, he complied, assisting her to remove her backpack. She opened it, pulled out the jewelry case, and set it on the table, slinging the bag over a chair. "Let me comm Georgia to tell her we've arrived."

She placed a finger to her temple, a gesture many people made when using their internal comms. "Georgia? It's Bassinae. I'm in interview room two. I've brought Cade." She paused for a moment. "Okay. See you."

Georgia came a few minutes later, wearing an elegant aubergine pantsuit with a pink pastel cloth over one shoulder. "Oh, my dear. You don't know how delighted I am that we were able to get my jewelry from Hugo. I can't thank you enough." She took Bassinae's hand in her own.

"Everyone was happy to help," Bassinae said.

Georgia grasped for her pearl pendant, encountering the pink cloth. She plucked it off and twisted it in her hands. ""Oh dear. I was helping out in the nursery. Thank you, too, for what you did for me. It seems silly to get so worked up over some jewelry, but it's a unique family heirloom. I don't have a daughter, so I'll be passing it on to my sister's child."

"You're welcome, ma'am."

Georgia moved to the table, placed the baby rag on it, and stroked the lid of the case before opening it to look inside. Once she'd seen the contents, she shut her eyes and clutched her pearl, heaving a big sigh. "It's all here." She turned, her face radiant. "I'd like to take the two of you out to lunch. My treat. And I'm going to wear my jewelry." She laughed. "I don't care that it doesn't match my clothes today. I'm wearing it. What do you say?"

"I think you deserve a celebration." Bassinae scooped Cade's hand into hers and looked up at him. "We'd love to."

"I'll drive. You can meet me in the garage," Cade said. He gave Bassinae a quick peck on the lips and left.

Georgia removed the gold studs in her ears and exchanged them for the scarab earrings in the case. She fastened the necklace on her own, but the bracelet was challenging.

"Let me," Bassinae said.

"That's your boyfriend. Very handsome."

Bassinae snapped the clasp closed and attached the safety chain. "He is. It's a new thing."

"I'm glad you've moved on. For so many of the women in the group sessions I've been in, the idea of being with a man terrifies them."

117

"I was like that. Time, lots of therapy, and the right person changed things for me." She plucked the brooch from the case and fastened it to Georgia's lapel. "There. Perfect. You're ready to celebrate."

Georgia gave Bassinae a tight hug. "Thank you, my dear." She lifted the case, tucking the gold earrings inside. "Let me put this in my locker and get my bag." She laughed and picked up the pink cloth. "And return this to the nursery."

* * * *

Georgia had insisted they eat at Finellies, an exclusive restaurant that had a months-long waiting list. It seemed Hugo was a partner in the business, so she could always get a table. She'd requested to be seated near the front of the house where an aviary with brightly colored birds fluttered and chirped.

It was one of those places that was so expensive they didn't bother putting the prices on the menus. Cade was finishing his steak, which he had to admit was the best piece of beef he'd ever eaten, when their pleasant lunch was interrupted by the curt voice of Hugo Bernard.

"Georgia. The maître d' told me you were here."

Bassinae's description of the man was spot on. He reminded Cade of a bulldog, an angry bulldog who was plowing through the dining tables straight for them. Georgia's eyes widened. Her back to him, her shoulders stiffened, and then she slumped when he stopped behind and to the left of her, his hand slapping onto the top of her high-backed chair next to her ear.

"It's time for you to come home, to stop this silly nonsense. You're making a fool of yourself." He glared at Bassinae and then at Cade. His face was a mottled red. "Who are you people? The ones who've been poisoning my wife against me? I won't have it. You should be ashamed of yourselves, coming between a man and his wife."

He slammed his hand on the chair back again. "Get up, Georgia. We're leaving."

Scooting away from the table, Cade said, "Mr. Bernard—"

"No." Cade glanced at Georgia, whose gaze was firmly locked on Bassinae. "Thank you, Cade. I'll handle this." She slipped from her seat, and for a moment Cade feared she was about to go with Bernard. "I'm not coming home ever again. I've left you, Hugo. You may expect divorce papers to be served in the near future. Now, please leave us alone. We were having a nice lunch until you showed up."

Bernard's face turned several shades darker. The choking sounds he was making worried Cade that the man was on the verge of having a seizure. When Bernard at last spoke, his words were strangled. Fists at his sides, he leaned forward, towering over Georgia.

"Where...did...you...get...that?"

He may never have hit his wife before, but there was always a first time. Cade got to his feet, stood at Georgia's back, and placed his hands lightly on her shoulders. She straightened. Her chin rose, and she lifted a hand elegantly to the scarab at her throat. "Do you mean this?"

Around them the other diners openly stared. The maître d' was nervously watching off to the side, checking over his shoulder, looking for someone with more authority who could intercede in the dispute.

"How did you get that jewelry?" Bernard seemed to have gained better control of himself. "Did these people help you steal it?" He gave Cade a look of hatred.

"Of course not, Hugo. You sold the set. Remember? I approached Tajan and asked if they'd represent me to the buyer. I had to pay a good deal more than the jewelry's value, but as you can see—" She brought her wrist up and displayed the bracelet for him. "I got what is rightfully mine back. And my lawyers assure me that since it is my family heirloom, I won't lose it in the settlement.

"I had planned to be generous and ask for only half of everything you own, but this little scene has changed my mind." She scanned the restaurant. "I think I'll take this. I do so love the food here. Frederick." She acknowledged the manager, who was now standing next to them. "Will you escort this gentleman from the premises? He's interrupting my lunch."

"She's leaving with me." Hugo was once again purple with rage.

Frederick looked from Georgia to Hugo, uncertain which side to take until Cade moved Georgia aside and took hold of Hugo's elbow. "I'll assist you, Frederick. I'm sure your clientele wouldn't appreciate the police disturbing their meal more than we already have. And I will comm them if you don't help me get this abusive bastard out of here."

His expression shocked, Frederick stepped forward. "Mr. Bernard, I believe it's time for you to go."

Shaking Cade's hand off his arm, Hugo spat his response at the manager. "I'm leaving." He glared at Georgia, aiming his animosity straight at her. "We'll see about this." Then he stomped from the restaurant.

"Thank you, Frederick. Well done," Georgia said.

Cade didn't agree, but he didn't say so.

"I think we'd like a slice of your famous strawberry cake and champagne. We're celebrating."

Frederick bowed. "Yes, ma'am," and scurried off to take care of the dessert.

"Let's sit and finish enjoying this delicious lunch."

Cade helped Georgia take her seat and resumed his own. Across from him Bassinae beamed at Georgia. "You stood up to him. That was amazing."

Her hand to her chest, Georgia said, "I didn't know I had it in me."

"Well, you did. I'm so proud of you."

Tears glistened in Georgia's eyes. She took hold of Bassinae's and then Cade's hand. "I couldn't have done it without people like you, complete strangers willing to help me." She gave Cade a scrutinizing look. "This woman"—she gave Bassinae's fingers a squeeze—"is special. But you know that. Take care of her the way a good man does. She deserves to stay happy."

Cade brought his gaze to meet Bassinae's. "I intend to do just that. As long as she'll have me." He looked at Georgia, lifted her hand, and kissed her knuckles. "Thank you."

The End
Thanks for reading! Please add a review where you purchased this book and let me know what you thought!

Find Cailin At

More about Cailin's books can be found on her website at http://cailinbriste.com.

Or join her newsletter at http://cailinbriste.com/cailins-newsletter-sign-up/.

Follow Cailin on:
Facebook: www.facebook.com/cailinbriste/

Pinterest: www.pinterest.com/cailinbriste/

Goodreads: www.goodreads.com/author/show/7413817.Cailin_Briste

Bookbub: www.bookbub.com/authors/cailin-briste 0GSX9QVW

Sons of Tallav Series

Shane: Marshal of Tallav

Shane Tiernan, the Beast of Tallavan aristocratic society, needs relief from the matriarchal rules that are destroying his life. His hope lies in a female submissive, newly graduated from a top sex school. From her resume, she seems perfect. Profile and real life collide when he arrives to collect her. He's stunned when he spots her vaulting over a bar and snatching up an ice chipper to defend herself against the giant who is chasing her. Her combination of warrior spirit and long-limbed curves fires his Dom imagination and the desire to bind her in his rope and have her under his complete control.

Adrianna Pacquin is sexually submissive, but don't cross her outside the bedroom. She's escaped the crime lord who plans to marry her once before. When it becomes clear he's still after her, she doesn't intend to get caught. A fortuitous decision to accept the contract of Tallavan Marshal Shane Tiernan promises safety until an attempt to murder him sets the pair on an investigation that will require complete trust in one another. With danger stalking their every step, the secrets they both hide could implode their blooming relationship and leave them exposed to their relentless foe.

Maon: Marshal of Tallav

Maon Keefe has always been told he's doomed to fail as a husband. He decides never to marry instead focusing on living life as a player and becoming a capable marshal of Tallav. When he is shot and the most-wanted criminal he's escorting escapes, he fears that his career, his one success in life, is doomed. Assigned to ferret out the cause of missing shipments for a VIP aristocrat, he meets Selina Shirley CEO of the House of Shirley. He finds himself inexplicably attracted to her despite her frumpy appearance. When he meets a hooded and masked, scorching hot Domme, Lasair, at his friend's BDSM club, he's torn between the two women. Both fire his imagination and call to his submissive nature. Either might be the woman to change him into successful husband material.

Selina Shirley organizes her life like she organizes her business, taking control of all aspects of each. She's concluded that she must marry to get an heir and that her future husband must be totally submissive. Mentored by the sector's most famous sadist, she learns what it takes to be a proper Domme. Then, hidden behind a hood and mask, as Lasair, she meets Maon and her instant attraction to his full submission at the BDSM club leads her to break her own rules and become involved with him. But he's also the marshal assigned to investigate thefts at her company. When his broad streak of protective alpha male comes into play, it obvious he's not a 24/7 submissive. To stick to her plan to marry the perfect husband, she must ignore her heart and dump Maon.

Rand: Son of Tallav – Due July 17, 2018

Randolph Meryon is a man no woman can resist despite the whip and title of sadist he brandishes. A pariah on his home planet of Tallav, he created a new life on Beta Tau, opening a kink club, The Whip Hand. The club is wildly successful, making him the most well-known and richest sadist in the sector. Old scandal comes roaring back into his life when his sister dies, and he's compelled to return to Tallav where his mother expects him to become guardian to his niece.

Jen O'Malley, reeling from the consequences of her own, more recent disgrace, must find employment. But shunned by the O'Malley family, her attempt to find work without their backing meets barriers on all sides. A position as nanny with the scandal-riddled Meryon family seems like a lifeline. She's relieved until she arrives at Briarcliff and falls under the spell of Randolph Meryon.

Did you love How to Steal the Pharaoh's Jewels?

Then you should read It Takes a Cat Burglar by Cailin Briste!

"The details are brilliant. Everything from Darcelle's training, to her trainers, to Sebastian are so wonderfully laid out that you'll feel as though you're a fly on the wall, watching everything happen." Leslie Obrien

"If you are looking for romance and excitement, you'll love this story!" Wendie Nordgren, sci-fi romance author

"I thoroughly enjoyed this book. It was full of intrigue and kept me guessing. This is only book one and I will be keeping my eyes opened for the next book in the series." A-N

When Darcelle Lebeau throws off the invisible chains that keep her bound to her family, she discovers a new vocation. Tempted to enter the illegal playground of a man she nicknames Matou, she becomes a cat burglar in training. Deeply ensnared with each task he entices her to fulfill, she fails to discover his identity and true intentions.

Sebastian St. Croix, a wealthy businessman, has a dark side. He's a thief, a cat burglar who steals art and historical objects. For one year, he trains Darcelle to become his assistant, remaining incognito, observing her from afar. His admiration grows along with his desire for her with every phase-one challenge she completes. Phase two will test the limits of his control. Hands-on personal training? Yes. Sex? No. With his sister's happiness at stake, nothing, not even the tempting Darcelle Lebeau, can interfere with accomplishing the biggest break-in of his career.

Buy Now to immerse yourself in the risky business of falling for a cat burglar.

The first in the A Thief in Love Romance series of novellas.

Read more at Cailin Briste's site at CailinBriste.com.

About the Author

Cailin Briste writes science fiction suspense romance. Her first series is set in the Tallavan sector of the Federation where the men of Tallav are the marshals that provide protection and justice to the planets in this far off the beaten path area of space. While fighting crime, they also must come to terms with the matriarchal system of their home planet, Tallav. Tricky because each is heavily involved in the BDSM lifestyle. Book one is her Dom, book two is her male submissive, and book three due out in July 2018 is her sadist.

Her second series, A Thief in Love Suspense Romance series, begins with a cat burglar who puts together a team to steal priceless art and antiquities from other thieves. Sebastian is a Robin Hood character whose Maid Marion is his equal on the rooftops of their futuristic city. The second in the series is the love story of two others on his team, Cade and Bassinae. Once again the team are breaking into someone's home to take back something that rightfully belongs to someone else, but this time they are also trying to stop a murder.

More books in each series are coming as is a new series about a pair of dragon shifters hatched from the same egg and the man they love, bounty hunter Brody Simmons.

Read more at Cailin Briste's site at CailinBriste.com.